Louis Enault, Linda da Kowalewska

Carine - A Story of Sweden

Louis Enault, Linda da Kowalewska

Carine - A Story of Sweden

ISBN/EAN: 9783337062477

Printed in Europe, USA, Canada, Australia, Japan

Cover: Foto ©Andreas Hilbeck / pixelio.de

More available books at **www.hansebooks.com**

CARINE

A STORY OF SWEDEN

By LOUIS ENAULT

TRANSLATED BY LINDA DA KOWALEWSKA

WITH ILLUSTRATIONS BY LOUIS K. HARLOW

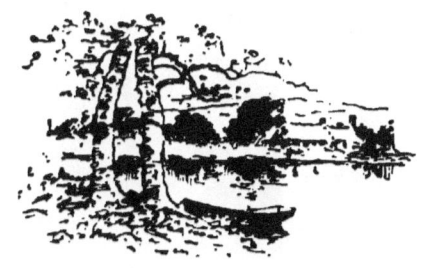

BOSTON
LITTLE, BROWN, AND COMPANY
1891

UNIVERSITY PRESS:

JOHN WILSON AND SON, CAMBRIDGE.

CARINE.

TOWARD the end of July, in the year 1856,
" La Walkyrie " (one of the finest packets of
the great Hamburg line) sailed across the Baltic Sea, and after a superb voyage entered the
fjord of Gothenburg.

It was nearly midnight; the sun descended
majestically into the depths of the Skagerrak,
leaving a golden light on the waves, — setting
slowly, as if loath to leave our hemisphere.
Arriving at the extreme point of the horizon,
where sky and sea seemed to unite, the golden
disk slowly sank beneath the waters, leaving

behind a mystic haze of mellow light. Ardent tints lingered in the west, of which the dominant colors were red and yellow blended in one harmonious cloud of most poetic tone, — the brilliant light above melting into a purplish hue, and above all the deep azure of the firmament, in which floated snowy clouds, taking all sorts of grotesque shapes. There were chariots with sparkling wheels, thrones of pale gold, and palaces with glittering spires and of most fantastic architecture. The wind arising from the sea dispersing them only to be replaced by still more ideal forms, they seemed like snowy silhouettes, so clearly were they defined by the deep blue background.

Scarcely had the last rays vanished, scarcely the last splendors effaced, scarcely had this bouquet of many colored flowers died away, when they were followed by tints of lilac ; and then o'er the eastern sky glided, with roseate hue, the first faint rays of dawning, — for in this far northern land on this night there had been

no darkness. All the passengers of " La Walkyrie " were standing in groups at the bow of
the vessel looking at the distant city which they
approached, and from which stretched two long

piers like welcoming arms to receive them. At
the foot of the bay, bathing its feet in the sea,
leaning against two granite mountains crowned
with fir-trees and surrounded by beautiful forests, the city of Gothenburg appeared before
them, bathed in the rosy light of the rising sun ;
this light, glancing over the waves, seemed to

send its rays not from on high, but from the ocean's depths from which it had just emerged.

The passengers were joyful, as one always is at a journey's end, however short; and this is especially so after a sea voyage. To feel one's feet again on terra firma, even if one's feet *do* step pretty high at first, is a great satisfaction. Most of these people were Norwegians, recognized by their heavy build and frank open countenances; they were returning from Bremen, Dantzic, and Lübeck, and were going on to Christiania after a halt at Gothenburg. There were also Swedes who had made "the grand tour of Europe" (as they call it in Stockholm), and now returned to their firesides with many souvenirs and curiosities. They were all fair complexioned, with light hair and blue gray eyes, changing from blue to gray like the sea with which they were so familiar; these were typical Norseman.

Very noticeable among these placid, fairhaired Scandinavians was a young man of a

decidedly different type; his dark complexion,
black eyes and hair, animated manner, and
quick step, made it impossible to identify him
with his more phlegmatic companions. He
was of medium height, slender and well-
formed; and the large-limbed Norwegians
could not help admiring his small hands and
feet. He went from one group to another,
laughing and jesting with all, talking in their
own tongue, and making so many droll remarks
and mistakes that he provoked smiles on all
sides. In the mean time they were passing
through a forest of sails, masts, and rigging, —
" La Walkyrie " opening a way, thanks to the
services of a skilful pilot, — and soon they
perceived the quay reserved for the packet
boats. The whistle blew noisily, the chains
rattled, and there was excitement on board;
the anchor sank in the shining sand, the small
bridge was thrown across, and the people
rushed on shore. The young stranger was
left alone. He looked at his watch and found
it was past midnight.

"This is no time," said he, "to pay visits. It seems to me the sun has lost his head; one knows not what to do in this singular country. I cannot distinguish night from day."

He leaned against a mast and watched his late companions descend; then he gazed a moment at the silent city. The morning (if one can give this name to the time that with us always belongs to the night) was charming; the air was clear and fresh as at daybreak in spring-time, the sun was not yet visible, the fjord was bathed in a glimmering light which threw out the piers in strong relief. All was silent.

Gothenburg slept!

In our climate, in the midst of our more exacting and energetic civilization, light to us means labor, and we know little of repose without darkness; therefore, to the inhabitant of more southern climes the first sight of these silent and deserted sunlit streets produces a strange, weird impression.

No sound could be heard, except the rippling and eddying of the sea, which penetrates almost to the heart of the city. The silence was funereal. A feeling of melancholy seized our traveller, and with this ennui; he realized that he was fatigued. Saluting with a yawn the Scandinavian sun and his first day under the sky of Sweden, he threw himself on some bales of cotton that were piled at the bow of the vessel, and fell into a profound slumber. When he awoke it was nine o'clock, and the city was already filled with noise and activity. He descended to his cabin, and after taking great pains with his toilet, ventured on the narrow bridge, and soon trod with joyful step the soil of Odin. At first he walked rapidly straight ahead, his elbows bent, shoulders up, nose in the air, eyes afar; he followed for a while the beautiful granite quay which runs in a straight line from the fjord to the mountain. After a brisk walk of ten minutes, drinking in the fresh air, he stopped and

asked a man whom he met to direct him to
a certain location; but he spoke so rapidly
and so brokenly that the man shrugged his
shoulders, and made a sign which signifies in
all languages, "I do not understand you" and

passed on, leaving our hero much chagrined,
for he had supposed that he spoke the language fluently. However, this young man was
not easily discouraged; so he tried it again,
and this time spoke slowly in a loud, distinct
voice. The man he addressed stopped, hat

in hand, smiling a little (no doubt at his strange accent), and made a courteous bow, regarding him with that charming good-will which inhabitants of far-off countries feel toward those who have braved the difficulties of their language.

After having received instructions, the young man changed his route, and leaving the straight line of the quay took a different direction; he soon arrived at the suburbs of the city (for it is much longer than it is wide), and paused before a fine substantial mansion whose massive door was ornamented with a burnished copper plate, which shone like gold, and which bore the name of M. Karl Johan Tegner, merchant. The stranger raised the knocker, which fell with a sonorous report on a carved bronze head, and presently the door opened, and he found himself in a large hall, the floor of which was covered with fir branches and sweet-smelling leaves. At the same time a young girl came out of the drawing-room and stopped

before him. They regarded each other a
moment without speaking. The maiden was
at home, — *she* had the right to wait; it was
the place of the new comer to speak. He
understood this, without doubt, for after a
moment of mute contemplation, at the same
time calling to mind all he knew of Sweden,
so as to give her a high idea of his erudition
and gallantry, he exclaimed, —

"How beautiful you are, Mademoiselle!"

"I am not beautiful," replied the young girl,
laughingly; "but *you* are a Frenchman." Her
face expressed enjoyment, good-humor, and
frank gayety, and she spoke (a little slowly,
perhaps, but with a pure accent) in the
pleasing idiom which is spoken between the
Seine and the Loire. When one is four or
five hundred leagues from his native land, the
sound of his mother-tongue is pleasing to the
ear and to the soul. Our hero did not speak
for a moment. "Am I mistaken?" said the
young girl. "Are you not a Frenchman?"

"At your service, Mademoiselle," replied he, bowing low to her. "I am French, Mademoiselle; or rather, I am a Marseillais. Do you understand?" he said gayly.

"But Marseilles is in France, I believe?"

"Without doubt, I am then French, as you said; and I am called Marius Danglade."

Marius paused as if to judge the effect of his name on the young girl.

"Marius Danglade," repeated the pretty Swede to herself, seeming to remember something.

"Have I the good fortune to be known to you?" said Marius.

"Known? No," replied she; "but somehow your name sounds very familiar. You say you are from Marseilles. Do you know the Swedish consul, M. Frederick Waldstrom?"

"Very well; I have a letter from him, and also one for M. Karl Tegner, who lives here."

"He is my father," said the young girl. "Be so kind as to come in the drawing-room. I will

let him know you are here." All this was said
gracefully, and with an air of perfect ease and
good-breeding.

Marius saw no difference in her manners
from those of the most well-bred French ladies.
He was not aware that the Swedes are called
the French of the North, and that the Swedish
women are noted for their elegance of manner,
serious education, and force of character. Following the young girl, he entered the salon;
then, ringing a bell, she gave a brief order,
which Marius did not understand, to the servant, who soon appeared with a tray, from
which she offered to her guest a glass of that
hydromel the Swedes call *mjod*. It is a liqueur
much esteemed by them, — sweet as honey, and
bitter as the beer from which it is composed.

Marius, before drinking, saluted her with a
mixture of politeness and cordiality, and re-
placing the glass on the silver salver, regarded
her with more attention than he had formerly.
She appeared to him to be about twenty years

old, — and he was not far wrong. The exclamation he had made on first seeing her was perhaps a little exaggerated, for her features were not regular enough for her to be considered in a strict sense a beauty; but she had many claims to the term. Her complexion was extremely fair, fresh, and rosy, and her expression brilliant. Added to this she was tall, and of an exceedingly beautiful form; her high forehead was crowned by an abundance of auburn hair, which curled lightly around her temples, and her dark-brown eyes were large and lustrous. All these charms dazzled Marius. He wished to continue the conversation, but could not think of a word to say, so he contented himself by drawing from his pocket his letters of introduction. Handing them to the young girl, he said, "Here are my credentials."

"You can give them to my father in a moment," she said smiling; "I hear his step in the room above. In the mean time be so kind as to give me some news of Madame

Waldstrom, — the lady who has given us the pleasure of your acquaintance. It seems to me she is becoming idle in France, for she seldom writes to me since she has been in Marseilles."

Marius had met the lady several times at balls. He assured the pretty Swede that her friend enjoyed herself very much in France, and that she found Marseilles the most charming city in the world.

"She ought to have taken the trouble to tell me so," said the young girl, smiling.

"She sent me to Gothenburg expressly to tell you," said Marius, gayly.

"Be seated then, Monsieur l'Ambassadeur."

She was still speaking when the door opened and gave passage to the majestic person of M. Karl Johan Tegner, — most honored citizen of Gothenburg, one of the greatest lights of the Consul du Banque, and one of the first notables of the Bank of Commerce. The young girl in a few words, and with the ease Marius had already admired in her, presented

the new comer to her father, and made known
to him the situation.

"M. Marius Danglade, welcome to Gothenburg, and to my house!" said M. Johan
Tegner, in much the same tone that Hamlet
took when he recéived his mother's guests.
Then he read the letter slowly, at times making expressive little nods. Folding it carefully
and putting it back into the envelope, he said :
"Waldstrom is one of my best friends; any
friend of his is mine also. We have expected
you for a long time, and we have interested
ourselves in you before knowing you. Your
name has been mentioned here more than
once. Has it not, Elfrida?" asked the honest
merchant.

"It is true, Monsieur. That is the reason
why your name seemed so familiar."

"All this is very well, my child," said the
merchant, looking affectionately at his daughter ;
"but instead of talking, have Monsieur Danglade's trunks sent to his room."

"It is necessary to know where they are," said she. "Monsieur, in coming here, had his cane in one hand, hat in the other. That is all I have seen."

"Mademoiselle is right," said Marius. "My modest artist's baggage is on board 'La Walkyrie.'"

"Artist, artist; it is not of an artist he has written me," thought Tegner. "May be it is a fancy of this young merchant to pass himself off as an artist. Of course I will say nothing; but I do not understand it.—Then," said he aloud, "you have left your trunks in your cabin?"

"Yes; and I am afraid I will not be permitted to bring them here without examination."

"That may be, young man; but *I* will have them brought here."

"Will it not be necessary for me to go?"

"At one word from *me*, Karl Johan Tegner, they would bring 'La Walkyrie' herself," said the merchant, with a gesture of proud confidence.

" I fear to abuse your hospitality."

" Have we the air of putting ourselves out for our guests?"

" No, indeed."

" Then, a truce to ceremony. We will be delighted to have you stay with us; one does not come here from the other side of the world — for we *are* a little far off — to stop at a hotel. When you are tired of us, young man, it will be time to think of going."

" Elfrida, see if our guest's chamber is ready."

Elfrida tripped out on the tips of her toes, light as a bird who condescends to walk on the earth, but who seems always ready to take wing.

" Même, quand l'oiseau marche, on voit qu'il a des ailes."

Five minutes later, a valet in livery announced that the French gentleman's chamber was ready.

"You are at home here," said the merchant, as he showed his guest upstairs, and ushered him into a large comfortable room containing one large window opening on to a charming view.

"How beautiful it is here!" cried Marius, looking out at the fir-crowned mountains.

"Try to amuse yourself, then; and stay a long time. I will give you the programme of the house: breakfast at ten, dinner at four, supper at nine, — and all with a very good appetite. Be prompt at your meals; it is the *one* thing I ask of you. I do not like to wait; that is my greatest fault. The rest of the time belongs to you."

After this little speech, delivered with much frankness and good-will, Monsieur Tegner closed the door, and left Marius alone to unpack his trunks at his leisure.

"What hospitable people these strangers are!" cried the young man. "It would be impossible to show more cordiality and con-

sideration ! Added to this the house is handsome and comfortable, and the view from this
window most beautiful. Those grand old
mountains seem to be posing expressly for me !
I have only to look out of my window to find
the most admirable models that a landscape
painter could wish for. I do not forget that
the daughter is charming ; if she were blond,
the lovely Elfrida would be perfection."

Marius was aroused from his pleasant revery
by some one knocking at his door. It proved
to be two sailors who were porters on board
" La Walkyrie," who brought his baggage,
and soon placed at the foot of his bed his
haversack and an enormous box of artists'
materials.

Chapter II.

Marius Danglade was a gay young man,
not ashamed of being young, and to whom
one could never dream of applying these
lines, —

" Donnez-moi vos vingt ans, si vous n'en faites rien ! "

for he employed his time in the best manner
possible. It is true, his twenty years were
twenty-five. He had first seen the light of
day in one of our most poetic cities, — a city
where almost every one has a sentiment and
taste for the fine arts, where nature has largely
endowed her citizens with aptitude to seize
and the faculties to express the beautiful. We

have already said Marius was a Marseillais.
Marseilles is filled with painters, musicians,
and poets, whose artistic productions reveal
remarkable talent; but in general its inhabitants make a pastime of art in their hours of
leisure.   Nature has been lavish, almost to
prodigality, to these Marseillais; and like all
inhabitants of southern regions, the more she
gives the less they dream to restore to her.
Like the peasants of this too fertile clime,
who are content to stir the soil with their feet,
and after sowing their seeds leave the rest
confidingly to the showers and the sunshine,
the Marseillais are too indolent to push to the
end that strong culture of the mind, without
which the human plant lacks the full perfection
of flower or fruit.

Marius was the son of a rich ship-owner,
who had a counting-house on the Cannebière,
a villa on the Prado, and a country-seat with
a *poste-à-feu* near the Gorges d' Ollioules.
He had shown from a tender age a great

talent for drawing. At six years he drew noses and ears; on his eighth birthday he presented an eye to his father. His parents were very proud of his talent, and his grand-parents said to themselves that one day their grandson would be a model cashier.

When he was fifteen they began to think he drew too much, and wished to take away his pencils and give him a pen. He gave up his pencils, but substituted a brush; one does not do sums in addition with carmine, ultra-marine and raw sienna! The family began to be alarmed. When he was eighteen, Marius declared that he would be an artist or nothing.

What a disappointment! It was not for this
his father had nurtured him so carefully. This
worthy man was a ship-owner; he had destined
his son for the same business; he possessed
capital in ten counting-houses which brought
him in a fine income,—was not *this* better than
to be a dauber of canvas? Menaces, prayers,
supplications were in their turn employed to
make Marius renounce his brushes and color-
box; but he had one of those decided voca-
tions which nothing can alter. He continued
to paint; he painted always, and he painted
well; he was successful even in his own
country. Every one praised his son's talent
to the ship-owner; this only augmented his
despair, — each compliment was like a dagger
in his heart.

"Our little Marius has great talent," said
to him one of his *confrères* at the bank.

"The little rogue will be the death of me!"
cried Monsieur Danglade, shrugging his shoulders mournfully.

Notwithstanding, when Marius had obtained the gold medal and a prize of five hundred livres in a competition opened by the artistic society of the Bouches-du-Rhône, his paternal vanity was a *little* moved ; but he was very careful to conceal it. When, the following year, Marius sold for two thousand francs to the Cercle des Phoceens, a little picture no larger than his two hands, the merchant concluded that, after all, perhaps the commerce of pictures might prove a good business for his son, especially if the rascal would always paint *large* pictures ; for he supposed the *larger* they were, the more money they brought.

After this, and in consequence of the declared intentions of his son, Monsieur Danglade — who loved Marius sincerely but in his own way — only resisted in form ; and after scolding a little more, gradually softened and finally surrendered, and finished by permitting this " wayward boy " to follow his *penchant.* What happiness for the young artist !

Yet our most excellent merchant was destined to undergo more tribulations. *His* son — the son and heir of a banker and shipowner — was not content to be a portrait painter; he preferred landscapes. Of all branches of the art of painting, landscape is the most delicate and the most reserved, and also most inaccessible to the *bourgeois,* whose unimaginative candor and simplicity demands something real and tangible. Nature only reveals her charms to the initiated, and willingly conceals them from industry and commerce.

Many persons, when they buy a picture, like to see men and women like themselves, sitting or standing, and gayly clad. They play, they eat, they drink, they kill, they die, they marry; in a word, they do those things which we are accustomed to see, and which we understand. This kind of painting is that which the artists, in their picturesque and imaginary language, name so well *chercher la petite bête. La petite bête* is that which best pleases *Monsieur Tout le Monde.* But to feel the mystic charm of daybreak or twilight in the great forests, the rushing and murmuring of the brook which runs under the willow's drooping branches, to perceive and feel Nature's most secret harmonies, one must be more than man: one must be a poet, — a rare species.

Marius could not content himself with being a painter, — aggravating circumstance! He was a landscape painter. And as if to mark the contrast between his birth and his destiny, in the midst of all these models, — arid, chalky, desolate, burned by the sun (nevertheless beautiful), which presented itself at each step in his native Provence, — this child of the South had a decided preference for northern scenery. A journey to Switzerland enchanted him. His delight was unbounded when he went from Martigny to Chamouni by Le Col de Balme. He divined the Alpine nature as it is given few men to divine.

He trembled with the black branches of the great fir-trees; the dazzling snow was full of charms for him; and he found a supreme pleasure in the vertigo one feels at the brink of an abyss. He even longed to descend into

the green depths of the sea of ice. He returned home in a state of febrile exaltation. He felt that he was not merely an artist with a brush in his hand; for he sought to penetrate the deepest secrets of Nature, and his inmost being thrilled with an enthusiastic love of the beautiful.

Marius's father was rich; and as every one knew he did not need money, they bought his pictures at a high price. Monsieur Danglade, *père*, was not avaricious, but he was a merchant, — that is to say, profit touched him; he began to believe that painting might, in some cases, be a *very* profitable business. The sight of the checks warmed his heart toward Marius; to tell the truth it had never been very cold toward his only son, and he was very glad of an excuse to show his affection.

About this time there came to Marseilles a friend of Monsieur Danglade. He was a lumber merchant from the North; one of the most influential men of Sweden. He had a counting-house at Stockholm, a manufactory at Motala for iron and steel, and lumber-yards at Christiansand, with a steam saw-mill. Monsieur Danglade and he had known each other many years, and had formed one of those friendly *liaisons* quite natural between merchants in the same line of business whose interests are the same. The old Swede took a great fancy to Marius.

"I have a beautiful daughter," said he to his friend. "As your son loves the fir-trees, the granite, and the snow, send him to us; he will be glad to go. As for the girl, *motus!* These things should come naturally, or not at all. If they do not fancy each other, there are plenty more beautiful maidens in Sweden; and they are as good as they are beautiful. Marriage will do great things for your son. He will then settle down, and will not be so restless."

The business was soon settled. They agreed that Marius should leave home toward autumn, and pass the winter in Sweden. Winter is the proper time to visit northern countries.

It was then spring-time; and the summer months are long under the burning southern sun. Marius, who did not dream of love, and whose mistress was art, asked nothing better than to go to Sweden, and spend his time in

the country fields. He had begun the grand
tour of Europe, — which every artist ought to
take, at least once in his life, — and was eager
to set off again immediately. But his father
was inflexible ; he loved his son after his own
fashion. He had made up his mind to this
separation, for he believed it would prove for
his good ; but he would not let him depart
until the appointed time. He engaged a Swedish professor for him, so that he might pay
court to the Swedish ladies in their own language, which is always an advantage.

Monsieur Danglade knew that Marius had
resisted all the seductions of Marseilles ; that
he seldom went to the *poste-à-feu* where the
young men of his age usually resorted for
shooting-matches, etc. ; and that he disap-
proved of the gallantries and dissipations of
his companions.

His father, prosaic as he was, comprehended
that there was something unusually noble and
pure in his son's character ; and he was secretly

proud of him, and respected him. He did not even hint of his marriage projects; so he signed his furlough for the first of July, and bade him God-speed.

Our hero, sufficiently ballasted with letters of credit, — and to such recommendations the business men of the North always pay due honor, — travelled through Europe slowly, loitering on the way; and, after several weeks' pleasant journeying, arrived at Gothenburg.

The address of the first letter of introduction we have already seen was to one of the most influential merchants of that city. His reception was most cordial, and Marius was prepared to enjoy everything.

Chapter III.

THE Tegner family breakfasted *invariably* at ten. Punctuality was M. Karl Johan Tegner's hobby; and for the right to the most beautiful of the three crowns of Sweden, he would not have consented to change for one instant the accomplishment of this important duty. The morning after our hero's arrival, he walked up and down the wide hall before his guest's chamber, and consulted his watch, which was regulated every three or four days; and when he saw that it only lacked one minute

3

of ten o'clock, he knocked at the door of the
young man's room. Marius immediately appeared, dressed and ready.

"You are punctual," cried his host. "Why,
this is a marvel! Nothing is so injurious as to
change one's meal hours. The stomach should
be respected, like misfortune! Come, let us
go down."

The clock on the staircase, the clock in the
hall, and the French time-piece in the drawing-
room (a time-piece of Boule brought from
France in the time of the Revolution, which
has scattered over the world our arts and our
ideas), and the summons of the dining-room,
sounded at the same time with a precision
which would have done honor to the marine
watch of an admiral. They had struck six
times when the two men put their feet on the
last step of the staircase. At the same moment, that most respectable lady Madame
Brigette Tegner appeared at the entrance of
the vestibule.

"Come, then, my dear," said the merchant, with the manner of a Louis XIV. *bourgeois;* "we have waited for you."

"I came out of church during the Reverend Oxen's sermon," replied Madame Tegner in

a meek voice, "and I do not think I am to blame."

"Come, then, to table," said her husband. "I hope Ulrica has been as punctual as we. My dear, in my haste I have forgotten to present to you our guest, M. Marius Danglade, a friend of that excellent Waldstrom, our consul at Marseilles."

"Monsieur, I am happy to meet you," said Madame Tegner, making a stiff and ceremonious bow.

Madame Brigette seated herself at the foot of the table, in a large wooden arm-chair, with a high back crowned with a canopy of elaborately carved wood, and with an air of dry dignity asked the young man to take the seat at her right. Then between them she placed a large prayer-book bound in black leather, whose well-worn corners attested constant use. Marius had hardly seen her yet; and as he loved to observe people, he profited by a moment when her attention was distracted to examine her hastily. She was a woman as tall as her husband was short, as thin as he was fat; she was tall, stiff, and straight, with strongly marked features. Her complexion was colorless, and the only expression she possessed was in her small gray eyes, which were keen and piercing, and shone with a hard cold light. Her hair, which cruel age had at the same time faded as well as thinned, might once have been auburn, if one could judge by the stray locks which occasionally escaped from her close black crape bonnet. She was dressed in a woollen robe of that sad color, to which the Carmelites have given their name, falling by a single plait from her shoulders to her feet; it looked like a meal sack. Altogether her appearance (despite the pleasant expression of her mouth when she smiled, which was rarely) was not very reassuring, and our young Frenchman felt somewhat chilled. She even had a bad effect on his appetite; but he soon learned not to mind the pious Brigette, who was always occupied with her religious duties, and who had very little to do with the housekeeping.

Besides, Marius had always before him, to nullify the depressing effects of the mother, the fresh young face of Elfrida, with all the careless grace and gayety of youth. This pretty creature went to and fro, making the tea, and attending to everything, without even tasting the raw fish, smoked meats, and other delicacies of no less rude digestion, which her parents seemed to relish so much.

"Do you never eat?" asked Marius.

"Sometimes," replied she, laughingly; "and I will keep you company in a moment. Will you not take one of these tartines and a cup of tea?"

It was she who served this perfumed beverage, and Marius looking at her rosy fingers and lovely hands found the tea of superior quality. He was not mistaken, for this was "caravan tea," brought overland through the steppes of Russia, which had not lost its delicate aroma by a sea voyage, for never had the iron and copper of a vessel mixed their perfidious odors with its subtile fragrance.

"And Carine?" cried Monsieur Tegner; "where is she? You well know that I do not enjoy my breakfast without her!"

"Behold," thought Marius, "a reflection,

which with these adorable mutton chops and this beef tongue, comes a little late ! "

" You think too much of that little one, and your sensibilities will kill you," said Madame Tegner with a seriousness so profound and a countenance so grave and impenetrable, that the most skilful physiognomist had been unable to decide whether this was a sarcasm or the expression of a sincere and solicitous affection.

Marius's eyes went from wife to husband without arriving at any conclusion. " Perhaps," thought he, " I shall be more successful with the daughter, who ought to be less dissembling," and he looked quickly at the young girl.

Elfrida was no less impenetrable than her honorable parents. She poured the cream into her tea, and seemed to pay the greatest attention to this difficult task, and her chief object seemed to be to see if she had sufficiently paled the Chinese nectar; but through her lowered eyelids, with that intuitive power of divination with which nature has endowed young girls, she felt that the stranger was watching her. She took from the table a cup of pink porphyry of Dalecarlia, which served for a sugar-bowl, and handing it to him said, "Will you have some sugar?" at the same time giving him a coquettish glance from her lovely brown eyes. Her expression was calm and serene, and Marius did not appease his curiosity in this quarter.

In the mean while Monsieur Tegner, who was of a positive nature, and was not the man to be satisfied with vague words when he took it into his head a reply was necessary, said severely, "I asked you," — and he glanced from the venerable Brigette to Elfrida, — "I asked you," repeated he, "*where* is Carine?"

Madame Tegner, who could dissimulate no longer, made a quick gesture of impatience, which was promptly suppressed, and looked down. As for Elfrida, a close observer might have remarked a trace of irritation in the fine and delicate arch of her eyebrows; but as her father had spoken particularly to her, she could no longer elude the question.

"Carine has already breakfasted," replied she, sweetly.

"Always the same!" said Monsieur Tegner in a grieved tone.

"Why do you wish her to change?" said his wife. "She is to-day what she was yesterday, and she will be to-morrow as to-day."

These remarks, questions, and replies, had been made quickly and in a low tone in Swedish, although French had been spoken before all through breakfast. Marius spoke the language tolerably well, but not well enough to understand perfectly this brief dialogue. Perhaps he would not have taken such an interest in the mysterious Carine had it not been for this; his curiosity was aroused by the reiterated questions of the merchant, the insufficient, and embarrassed replies of his wife and daughter, which seemed to throw a little

restraint over all, as each one hastened to leave
the table. Madame Tegner gave the signal
by taking her book, which she placed under
her arm; then raising herself stiffly from her
chair, like an automaton worked by springs,
she left the room, followed by Elfrida.

Tegner was much chagrined by the unfortunate result of his remarks, and hastened to
console himself with a little glass of old rum;
then making the tour of the room two or
three times, to gain the thread of his ideas
interrupted by the copious breakfast he had
swallowed, as one unites the ends of the
transatlantic cable broken by a tempest, and
putting his hands on Marius's shoulder, he
said, —

"Young man, you are as free as a bird in
the air, as a fish in the water. The city is
pleasant, the country is beautiful, and the roads
are good. I wish I could accompany you and
do the honors of my country; unfortunately, I
am obliged to make much money, and I work

harder than any two of my clerks. Do you
wish a guide? I cannot promise a good
one."

"Keep him, then," said Marius, gayly. "I
do not like a courier. I make voyages of dis-
covery, which amuse me infinitely. I am capable of discovering that you have a church, a
prison, and a bank. Do not fear; I will amuse
myself all day."

"Very well, my dear boy, on condition that
your day is finished at four o'clock; for at
four o'clock and thirty seconds we shall be
seated at the dinner-table. You have seen
that I allowed a little delay at breakfast, but
in regard to dinner I am inflexible; pass that
time, and your punishment will be severe."

Before leaving the house Marius looked for
Elfrida; but she was nowhere to be seen.
She had retired to her room to sew or to
study; for although the Swedish ladies give
their evenings willingly to hospitality, polite
conversation, and honest familiarity, they re-

serve at least the greater portion of their days
for the cultivation of their minds, and for the ·—
performance of household duties.

The young Frenchman occupied the whole
day, which seemed very short, in roaming
about the city. It is a rare enjoyment,
always appreciated by an artist, to find one's-
self in the midst of a foreign country, where
everything is new, strange, and surprising, and
where each step leads to the unknown. Marius, with artistic instinct, sought everywhere
new types of beauty or ugliness. He followed
an elegant form across the street; he walked
a half mile to meet again a beautiful blonde
with floating hair under a large hat. All this
without the least thought of wrong; his admiration was purely artistic. A man, provided
that he was well built, that he had a figure
which would look well on canvas, was as
much the object of his minute examination
and systematic research as the most beautiful
woman. With Marius passion had not yet

awakened; it was the artistic sense that dom-
inated his spirit.

The day passed rapidly, like enchantment;
without leaving the city, Marius had enjoyed
himself greatly. He saw, he lived, he studied,
and he learned; he found everything attractive,

and everything he saw charmed him. Gothenburg is truly a pleasant city, admirably situated,
full of life and movement, attracting all the
neighboring population as the centre of commerce, and presenting to the traveller numerous
samples of different races, and a foretaste of

Swedish civilization which he will find later on at Stockholm, its brilliant capital.

Our Marseillais would have gladly passed the rest of the day wandering around the city; but he had constantly on his mind the urgent request of his worthy host to be punctual at dinner. He had faithfully promised this magnificent diner to be prompt, and he did not wish to give his host a bad opinion of his good breeding, on the first day at least. On passing a church he looked at the dial, the hand of which pointed to twenty minutes before four. He was not sure of his way, and as he did not wish to lose any time asking people who might find his Swedish unintelligible, he hailed one of the six public carriages of Gothenburg and pronounced the name of Tegner. The driver on hearing it smiled knowingly, and nodding, as if to say, "I understand," whipped his horses; and after a rapid drive of five minutes through the narrow streets, Marius found himself before the substantial

mansion of the honorable merchant, easily
recognized by its granite corners, its salmon-.
colored walls, and its light green outside
window-blinds. He paid the man liberally,
laughing to himself at his narrow escape, and
entered the house.

Chapter IV.

THE house had taken on an air of festivity.
There were fresh leaves and sweet-smelling
herbs on the floor of the wide hall; there was
sage, thyme, lavender, rose-leaves, and other
fragrant herbs new to Marius. An appetizing
odor from the kitchen spread itself from cellar
to garret; the stew-pans smoked on all the
stoves; the butler carried in a basket filled with
bottles of all sizes; and the majestic Ulrica
showed her importance before the vast fire-
place, where three stories of roasts were baking
at the same time.

The honorable Karl Johan Tegner stood with his hands crossed behind his back, in a satisfied manner. He went from one thing to another, giving everything the finishing touch; he tasted the sauces and the salads, and laid out in a row on the vast sideboard the bottles brought from the cellar, in the order he wished them to be served, and himself placed on each napkin the name of the distinguished guests who were to dine with him.

"A la bonne heure!" cried he on seeing Marius. "Behold a punctual man! But be tranquil; before forty minutes we will eat a soup of swallows-nests, which has been sent to me expressly from Holland, and which will be served by the hands of no less a person than Madame Karl Johan Tegner."

"You are superb!" cried Danglade, regarding the brilliant cravat, the chamois waistcoat with large revers, and the maroon coat with golden buttons of the merchant. "Is it then a fête? Are you going to marry your daughter?"

"Not yet," said Tegner, winking his eye.

"Then you have the viceroy, the admiral, the general, for your guests?"

"You will soon see," said Tegner, strutting like a peacock, which proudly displays its brilliant plumage.

"Well, as it is thus, I will go to my room and make myself worthy of the illustrious company."

"Ha, ha! make yourself handsome!" cried the jolly host; "every one cannot be that."

When Danglade reappeared in a costume of which the elegant simplicity contrasted perhaps with the gorgeous apparel displayed by Tegner, he found five or six men in the salon. The merchant named them successively, — the president of the bank; the commander of a squadron of artillery, charged with the coast defence; several wealthy merchants of the city. The young Frenchman was received with that courtesy and good-will which all Swedes feel for us.

As the guests had all arrived, the folding
doors opened, and Madame Tegner appeared,
followed by Elfrida. The elder lady had not
as usual her prayer-book under her arm ; but
it was clearly to be seen that she missed it,
for at times she pressed her elbow to her side
as if to prevent its falling, and seemed embarrassed on not finding it in its accustomed
place. The gray woollen gown was replaced
by a robe of violet silk, the shape of which was
the same as a sack ; it hung in shapeless folds
around her bony figure. It was evident that
crinoline had not yet reached Sweden, or else
the pious lady objected to it on religious
grounds.

Happily Madame Tegner had a lovely
daughter, who dressed well. Whether she
had a particular reason for appearing more
beautiful than usual this evening we cannot
say ; but it is certain that she was so charming
that the gentlemen of the party could not refrain from an exclamation of admiration when

she appeared before them. Their praises
were merited. It was hardly possible to look
fresher, or more like a lovely half-blown rose
from which the dew had never been shaken.

Her brilliant eyes shone like two black diamonds, her forehead gleamed like polished
white marble, and her lovely complexion was
as transparent as alabaster.

Perhaps in Paris, where capricious fashion
exercises always an empire as ridiculous as it

is absolute; at Paris, where a thing is out of
fashion to-day for the simple reason that it was
the fashion yesterday; and where the first title
to be is of not having yet been, — at Paris one
might have considered this costume of Elfrida
old-fashioned. It was simply a velvet spencer
of a light green color, fitting perfectly her
charming figure, open at the neck, revealing
her beautiful swan-like throat, and ending with
three little sashes over a white, hooped silk
skirt. This might have been the fashion of
1820; but for Marius it was all the same. In
1856 this costume certainly was not worn
at Paris or at Marseilles; but the dress
was pretty, and exceedingly becoming to
Elfrida.

In the mean while our worthy host had not
forgotten the dinner; and after his guests had
sufficiently admired his daughter's beauty, and
paid tribute to her good taste, — which pleased
the father, for it tickled his paternal vanity, —
he hastened to remind them: "All this is

very well," said he, "but my daughter is modest, and the dinner is getting cold."

Elfrida then rang a bell, when a servant in full livery entered the room bearing a large tray loaded with sandwiches, in which smoked fish took the place of our ham or tongue, and with little glasses of white brandy distilled from potatoes. Each one ate a sandwich or two, and swallowed his glass of this beverage, which Marius found frightful; after which they passed into the dining-room, where most of the guests showed veritable prowess.

Our young friend had been superseded in the place of honor at Madame Tegner's right by two gray, bald, and portly functionaries; but as he was placed between Elfrida and her jolly old father, the change was a most agreeable one to him, and he did not dream of complaining. He spoke often in French to his lovely neighbor, much to the displeasure of their *vis-à-vis*, — a young merchant, whose appetite suffered from ineffectual attempts to hear fragments of their conversation, of which unfortunately the meaning escaped him more than the words. He was a handsome young man with thick red hair, light-blue eyes, carrying lightly his thirty-four years, and answering to the name of Frederick Brask. He had long sighed for the fair Elfrida, but they were not yet *fiancés.*

After a while, when the edge of their appetites was somewhat appeased, and when the wines of France and Germany had elevated their spirits, the host rose, and holding a bottle in one hand, and in the other a champagne glass of Bohemian ware, cracked to imitate ice, — a glass so rare and beautiful that it seemed to improve the piquant aroma of the generous and insidious liquor, — "I drink," said he, "'fraternity' with the young Frenchman Marius Danglade, whom I have had the pleasure to present to you this evening."

· "Provided that it be not *paternity* that we drink together," murmured Frederick Brask.

Elfrida lightly shrugged her shoulders; but Tegner heard nothing, or feigned not to hear; for filling the glass of Marius and his own, and locking his right arm in the left arm of his guest, they raised at the same time the glass to their lips. This ceremony is called in Sweden "Drinking fraternity," and is a sacred tie between two men. All the guests came in their turn and touched their glasses to that of the young Frenchman. Only one thought best to refrain, and remained aside; this was Frederick Brask, who observed all the details of this little scene with an uneasy attention. Marius showed his good breeding by not noticing this apparent slight, which seemed to mortify Elfrida very much.

By this time their vast libations had begun to take effect, and would have sent under the table long ere this less experienced drinkers. Many of the guests, no doubt, on returning home found the streets very narrow and the walls very unsteady.

When they had all gone, Tegner, whose tongue was a little thicker than usual, said in that deep grave voice in which a man speaks after drinking, " Where then is Carine? "

"She is in her room," replied his wife, coldly, who during dinner had drunk nothing but water.

Elfrida looked toward her mother, but said nothing. As for Tegner, he arose, not without leaning heavily on the arm of his chair, and went into the other room.

Chapter V.

"WHO *is.* this Carine?" Marius asked himself, entering his chamber after his host had wished him "Good-night and golden dreams." "Is there then a tragedy being played in this patriarchal family? Am I at the entrance of a mystery of Udolpho? This frank and honest appearing father, is he an ogre, with an appetite for human flesh, and to whom is served infants for supper? The austere Brigette, this shy Puritan, does she conceal under an aspect of piety a cruel nature, persecuting innocence and tyrannizing over weakness? and, last, this pretty Elfrida, — does she get her rosy cheeks only by sucking human blood? Is she a vampire? And for the unlucky stranger whose evil star has led him into this house, ought he to barricade his room, bolt the door, and put some loaded pistols near his bed before sleeping? Come," said he, "all this is absurd! How do I know who this Carine is? She may be a nervous aunt, a cousin in disgrace, or some unfortunate girl. I will not bother my head with the affairs of others. Behold, a voyage begun under happy auspices, and my first day in Sweden has been well occupied."

Marius then looked at his watch for the tenth time that day (he was becoming methodical like his host), and was astonished to find that it was past eleven. It was still daylight, and he thought that if he went to bed he could not sleep a wink, as he was not accustomed to sleep by daylight. So he took out his sketch-book and began to sketch from

memory a beautiful tree he had noticed during
his morning ramble. He went vigorously to
work; but like the oaks and the laurels of the
forest of Armida, the tree opened its trunk to
reveal a female form; its branches became
beautiful arms, and its spreading roots changed
to little feet. The head only was always lost
in the leaves; and if the beautiful Elfrida herself had been looking over his shoulder she
could not have accused his crayons of im-
pertinence.

Suddenly Marius threw down his work, like
an unfinished essay unworthy to see light.
"This champagne is no good," cried he;
"it is not true Cliquot, but a detestable imi-
tation. My hands tremble, my face is flushed,
and I feel horribly. This cooking with so
much red pepper burns my very entrails; I
am always drinking to quench my thirst, and
as the proverb says, 'Who has drunk will
drink.'" He then poured out a glass of fresh
water, took off his dress-coat and put on a

soft shooting-jacket that he usually wore in his studio, rolled a cigarette deftly between his fingers, and opened the window.

The sky was of a deep blue, and the light of infinite softness. The eye travelled far in the distance. For Marius, who was accustomed to the brilliant southern sun, this was delightful, and he gave himself up to the charm of the northern sky, so blue and opaline. Nervous, like all artists, sensitive as a woman, accessible to all the impressions of the exterior world, his feelings were instantly touched with an ineffable tenderness, which closed around him. This calm, this silence, this delicious air, these ethereal lights that softly bathed the sleeping earth, — all this aroused his inmost being. His window opened from the floor on a large balcony, which commanded a beautiful and extensive view of the mountains. He leaned his elbows on the iron railing of the balcony, near which he had rolled his arm-chair, and looked at the beautiful landscape which lay

before him. Then perceiving that the balcony ran around the house, and made what
the architects call a *retour d'équerre*, he
advanced toward the part which overlooked
the flower garden. But at the moment when
he turned the corner which separated one
façade from the other, he was struck with astonishment; for at the entrance to a bower
formed by clematis and hop-vines, whose
climbing shoots were interlaced around some
pine-trees (forming a natural bower), he saw
a woman! She was so motionless that she
might have been taken for a beautiful statue.
Leaning on the massive trunk of a linden-tree,
her chin in her left hand, her bare right arm
falling its full length, one foot advanced,
her head bent as if listening, — one would
have said that she listened with all the forces
of her being, and that not the slightest noise
floating in the air could escape her. But
reassured by the silence and calm which
reigned around her, she started forward, and

coming out of the shadow entered into the full light. Marius, who had an artist's eye, could see her perfectly, as in daytime.

She was a young girl, who seemed to be about eighteen years old; she was not quite so tall as Elfrida, and she did not seem to have the force or the vigor of the blooming maiden who had only that morning welcomed him as her father's guest. This maiden appeared delicate almost to weakness; she was slender, frail, and pliable as a reed, and as easily broken. The distance did not as yet permit Marius to distinguish her features very clearly, but they appeared to be small and regular. She was bareheaded, and her blond tresses fell over her shoulders in a golden cloud nearly to her feet. She wore a strange costume, with which he was not familiar. It was that of the Dalecarlia fisherwomen, who perform at Stockholm (the Venice of the North) the same office that the gondoliers there perform on the grand canal, and in the lagoons of the beautiful and unfortunate city of the Adriatic.

Marius, charmed with this adventure, remained immovable and mute. He scarcely breathed, so fearful was he of frightening away this lovely vision; and he remained so closely pressed against the wall that he looked like a bas-relief set in Tegner's house. The young girl - took a few steps in the direction of the garden-walk, then paused, and seemed to sink into a deep revery; she remained some time in this position, the soft light enveloping her form, and enabling Marius to examine her more attentively than he had yet done. Completely assured that she was alone, the lovely phantom shook back her floating hair, then advanced into the garden and paused beside a bed of pansies and forget-me-nots, — those little blue flowers that the Germans have made the emblem of remembrance. She seated herself almost opposite the balcony where the young man was concealed behind a pillar. This time

the artist could contemplate the apparition at
his ease, and almost as well as if she had been
in the drawing-room.

The young girl was indeed charming, despite
an expression of profound melancholy im-
printed on her youthful features. Danglade,
enthusiastic as a poet, never remembered having seen before a face so beautiful and be-
witching. All her movements were as graceful
as a wild fawn's, like one who had always lived
near Nature, and far from the world. She was
occupied in arranging the flowers she had just
plucked. With great care she assorted the
colors and combined the shades; her task was
absorbing, and she gave it her undivided attention. Marius followed the motion of her light
fingers, — now breaking off the stalks, now
pruning the leaves, and arranging the flowers
with exquisite taste. The oblique light struck
her face, and brought out in strong relief her
beautiful head, so purely modelled, and her
low broad forehead, white as the newly fallen

snow; and under her snowy brow, under the long dark eyelashes, her eyes, which she raised several times to the heavens, had the dark-blue tint of wet violets. Her profile was poetic, correct, and fine, and had the ideal pallor of marble.

Upon a man like Marius, easily exalted and prompt to admire, such a vision at such an hour and under singularly romantic conditions, naturally produced a lively impression. Mute, immovable, retaining almost breathless all his soul in his eyes, which he could not detach from this beautiful face, he contemplated the little scene with that profound and absorbing attention which engraves forever such scenes on the memory.

Soon the young girl arose; her task was finished. Perhaps the chill of the night had fallen on her, for a slight tremor shook her frail form. For a moment she stood still; then she looked at her bouquet, untied the ribbon with which it was fastened, and separat-

ing the flowers she had just arranged with so
much patience and care she threw them into
the deep foliage near her.   Then brushing back
a long curl which had fallen over her brow, she
gave a furtive glance around her, and hearing
a window open and a voice calling, " Carine !
Carine !" she ran across the walk and entered
the house.

Chapter VI.

MARIUS looked longingly after her; then lightly recrossed the balcony and returned to his room without having attracted any one's attention.

Safe in his chamber, Marius was more agitated and perplexed than ever. Nevertheless, he had seen Carine! This name which had so interested him, and of which he had been dreaming all day, did not belong to an ugly old woman, but to the most charming creature he had ever seen. Carine was a young and lovely girl; she lived under the same roof, near him,—perhaps she was in the next room! But *who* was she? Was she Elfrida's sister, Monsieur Tegner's daughter? Was she a stranger sheltered by this benevolent Tegner? Was she a culpable child, under punishment? This seclusion to which she was condemned, was it voluntary? All these and many more questions he asked himself. His very soul was agitated with the intense ardor of his youthful nature, yet he could not solve the problem. I do not believe he slept much that night; but I do know that never before had he had such dreams.

The next morning he awoke early, and quickly dressing himself descended into the garden. As yet the whole household slept. All was fresh and quiet; indeed, the air was so clear and invigorating that it acted like wine upon our hero's spirits. He seated himself on the same bench where the night before he had seen Carine (it seemed natural for him to prefer the seat she had so long occupied) ; then making sure that he was alone, he entered the thicket, and bending, picked up some of the flowers scattered here and there by the lovely vision of the night. Calmer now, and his head refreshed by the sweet morning breeze, Marius returned to his room, threw himself dressed on the bed, and fell into a profound sleep.

Our hero awoke a little late, and remembering his host's hobby about being punctual, made a hasty toilet, not wishing to injure the best regulated stomach in Gothenburg, and was rewarded by entering the dining-room one quarter of a second before Tegner, — who believed that he paid his young guest an unequalled compliment by telling him that he had never met a watch or a Frenchman who kept time better than he. Marius was not endowed with extreme penetration, but he could not help seeing a cloud on the face of the honest merchant; for after wishing him good-morning very cordially, Tegner seemed to pay no further attention to the young man for some time, but walked up and down the large room with his hands crossed behind his back, seeming to be thinking out or trying to solve some difficult problem. He even went once or twice to the vestibule, then to the street door, and also to the one that led to the garden, as if looking for some one. At last, seeing that it was nearly ten o'clock, and that the majestic Ulrica, with an important and busy air, began to lay the warm plates on the table, Monsieur Tégner armed himself with a sudden resolution, and taking his guest's arm silently invited him to join his promenade. After a moment of silence he coughed and said, —

"I have only known you since yesterday; nevertheless, it seems to me that we are old friends, and I feel a confidence in you. I believe that we are destined to pass some time together, and you will do me a favor if you will look on this house as your own. It is better, therefore, that I should apprise you of something that you are certain to find out sooner or later for yourself."

After saying this, Tegner was silent for a moment; but as Marius said nothing, he coughed once or twice and continued.

"You already know," said he in a low voice, "my wife and my daughter; but Elfrida and Madame Tegner are not all of my family; you will see another person. If in her words or actions you remark anything singular, you will do well to take no notice of it whatever."

Marius was visibly agitated by these words; he made a gesture of assent and replied, "This person — you call her Carine, I believe?"

"Ah, you know her name?"

"Did you not mention it before me twice yesterday at table?"

"Oh, yes, I believe I did. Well, Carine is not — "

M. Karl Johan Tegner did not have time to finish his sentence; for just then the door opened, and Madame Tegner entered the

room, followed by two young girls. The first
was Elfrida, with whom Marius already felt well
acquainted, and who greeted him cordially,
giving him her hand, which Marius pressed
gently à l'Anglais. (Our ancestors kissed the
hand of lovely woman; we shake it!) The
other girl, who seemed to be a year or two
younger than Elfrida, kept a little behind Madame Tegner, — it seemed as if she wished to
hide in her shadow. The merchant hesitated
a little before presenting her to his guest; then
taking her by the hand said simply, "Carine,"
without other designation.

Marius had already recognized the lovely
nocturnal vision; but he had only seen her the
night before at a certain distance, and could
not now refrain from looking at her with much
curiosity, — which did not surprise Monsieur
Tegner, as he attributed it to his previous
remarks, as well as to the singular though
picturesque dress worn by Carine. She wore
the Dalecarlian costume, which was so striking

and peculiar that, thought the honest Tegner, an artist would naturally examine it with attention. As for Elfrida, she followed with an interest no less lively the impressions which successively manifested themselves on the mobile and frank countenance of the artist; but Marius, feeling himself thus observed, immediately threw over his face an impenetrable mask, promising himself, however, to lose no occasion whatever of continuing his observations.

As for the lovely *inconnue*, she bowed to the stranger, in whom she took no interest, with an air of perfect indifference; and without further notice or thought of him, she seated herself at what seemed to be her accustomed place at the table, at the left of Monsieur Tegner.

Marius was not only an artist, he was a man of the world, used to the best society. He understood instantly that he was in a difficult position; that every one was restless, and that his presence aggravated this feeling. Indeed, he mentally resolved to beat a quiet retreat as soon as possible; but for the present he must not appear ill at ease or constrained, thereby annoying his entertainers. Therefore he drew on all his resources of wit and good-humor: he made gay and witty speeches; he explained the theory of the *bouillabaisse* to Tegner, àpropos to a certain sauce served with the trout; he talked religion with the austere Brigette, and discussed the latest Parisian fashions with Elfrida; he even tried to attract Carine's attention, but was finally obliged to admit to himself that the beautiful unknown had not even the slightest suspicion of his intentions. Once or twice, however, if he had observed her more closely, he might have seen a faint smile appear at the corners of her lips without daring to spread on her serious mouth. He was almost sure that she understood French as well as the rest of the family; for while the Norwegian, forgetful of France, turns more and more to the side of England, the Swede remains faithful to our language and literature. Once,

for an instant, Marius thought he caught the
eye of this dreamer ; but she turned her head
quickly, and dropped her eyelids promptly, —
not soon enough, however, for the artist
had time to look into her soul, where he
divined a profound sadness. During the remainder of the time the young girl appeared
entirely indifferent to all that passed around
her ; and our hero, fearing to annoy the family,
appeared not to notice her. He profited however by the revery into which she sank to admire her natural elegance and exquisite grace,
which greatly enhanced her beauty ; he found an
infinite charm in her profound and fleeting air
of sadness, and in her delicate and transparent
complexion. She seemed a maiden expressly
created to love and to suffer. Although she
had spoken but few words, her voice seemed
to Marius to possess a depth of *timbre*, and at
the same time it was melodious, penetrating,
and pure ; even when she spoke softly, this
charming voice had that peculiar sympathetic

quality which is so rare that one can describe it only in a word, *voix sympathique*, and the sound seemed to come from afar. Marius noticed in the maiden an air of dejection; and she looked so very frail and spirit-like that it seemed as if she said in a low voice, "Do not approach me, for a great misfortune has happened to me, and I am as one apart!"

Thanks to the unheard of efforts made by Marius to keep up the conversation, the ice was broken; one felt no longer constrained, and they all seemed to wish to atone to their guest for the temporary coldness which had prevailed. Tegner was radiant, for he had feared that this gloom might impair his digestion, and his usual beaming smile appeared on his face when his dear Elfrida prepared his tea as of old. Carine, who had not even tasted the wine or beer, drinking only water, now quietly left the room, and seemed to carry with her the last trace of anxiety and apprehension; for she had done nothing to justify their fears, and a general feeling of relief prevailed.

After breakfast Marius took his sketch-book and wandered out into the country, under the pretext of study; his real motive was a desire

to be alone. Was he truly alone in the midst of this Nature, so grand, rugged, and melancholy; these mountains covered with heather, and these granite rocks crowned with the eternal verdure of the firs? Did he not carry with him an image, which time had hardly as yet graven on his soul, but which passed and re-

passed before his eyes? This question he
alone can answer. All that we as his historian
know, is that until now he had only known one
type of beauty, — that of the southern brunette, with dark complexion, brown eyes, hair
black as ebony, or lustrous blue-black like
a raven's wing. God forbid that ·I should
decry the beauty of the women of Marseilles!
There are many families in Marseilles where
this peculiar type of beauty is a heritage from a
remote ancestry. The splendor of their oriental charms is rarely outdone elsewhere in Europe; at least nowhere can be found. such
perfect mouths, such pure profiles, or brows so
finely modelled, — in a word, living heads
resembling so faithfully the immortal beauty of
the statues and medallions of Sicily and Greece.
But brilliant as is brunette beauty, it has only
one note; and when one has sufficiently sung
of it, one remembers that the scale complete
has seven notes, without counting the sharps
and flats.

Independently of this prestige of the unknown, so full of seduction for a nature young and susceptible to all the emotions of life, Carine was for Marius a revelation, — a revelation of the blond type, which was that of Eve, of Venus, and of Helen of Troy, and of almost all the celebrated heroines which artists and poets have made immortal. She was also to him a revelation of northern beauty, which appeals more to the soul than to the senses, — so pure that it seems immaterial, like the icy glaciers which are at the same time cold and brilliant, and which give to the lakes in which they are reflected their limpidity and transparency. At home Marius had been so occupied with his art that he had no place for other seductions, and this was the first time his soul had been aroused. He thought of Carine's beautiful face, her rosy lips, her perfect mouth, her snowy, satin-like complexion, her long light hair, fine as spun silk and golden as amber. Would she ever think of him? Alas! he feared

not; she had not even looked at him! He
wished to be alone; he had wished to plunge
even into the bosom of the mountain, to be
alone all this long day under the shadow of the
firs and beeches. He desired to be far away
from the world, and for a week or two to flee
from Tegner, Elfrida, and Carine herself, to
commune with his own soul and with Nature.
At last he tried to think of something else;
and as his was a brave nature, he courageously
aroused himself, took his brushes, worked
with ardor, and made a study which occupied
half the day. "He who labors suffers not;"
"activity of spirit makes sentiment sleep;"
and his heart had an intermission. But when
his work was finished, and he was closing his
portfolio, he said to himself, "If she only
loved painting!" Then he hastened to return to the city, bounding like a chamois
over the crevices in the rocks. When he
saw the houses of the city his chest heaved,
and he paused. "Down there," said he, look-

ing at Tegner's house, — "it is there *she* lives!"

They dined that day *en famille.* No one came, to our hero's great joy; for he felt quite incapable of carrying on a polite conversation with strangers, answering questions as to "how he liked Sweden," and if he "expected to remain long." The weather was warm, the evening charming. After dinner Tegner proposed a walk in the country; but his wife, who soon retired to say her prayers, pleaded fatigue, and they remained in the garden.

It was a very pleasant, quaint old garden, but rather small, like all city gardens. When they had sufficiently surveyed its length and breadth, Tegner, who was no walker, seated himself on the marble bench where Carine, the preceding night, had remained so long. This was near the house, opposite a beautiful porphyry vase, which although not quite so large as that of Rosendal (which is the special admiration of all visitors at Stockholm) was no less worthy of figuring in the park of a prince.

No one talked, and each individual seemed plunged in revery. Does not melancholy seem the natural attribute of certain hours? The three women were seated in rustic chairs, the men at each end of the bench. By chance Marius was placed near Carine. He greatly desired to speak to her, but a certain respectful fear withheld him. It seemed as if she was enveloped in an atmosphere of sadness, and that it would be almost a profanity to address her in the polite language of society. Little by little the pure and chaste beauty of the young Swede had calmed the ardor of his southern blood; he wished to respect this snow maiden. Looking down he perceived in the grass at his feet a tuft of withered myosotis and a sprig of thyme, — waifs from the bouquet of the past evening. He picked them up and inhaled their perfume, — for even when crushed certain flowers retain their sweetness; and when he was certain that he had attracted Carine's attention he turned to her quickly, and showing her the flowers, pointed to the balcony that had served for an observatory. Her hands trembled, and she blushed deeply. It was the first sign of emotion that he had observed in her; however, it was promptly repressed, and an instant after Marius had only an alabaster statue at his side.

Soon after this they withdrew to the drawing-room to wait the tea-hour, — of which our worthy host made a veritable lunch with all sorts of comfortable and savory accompaniments.

(hapter VII.

THE place to see the Swedes at their best is in the drawing-room. In general this room much resembles that of the English, — little luxury, little useless superfluities, and not so many of those cumbersome curiosities with which our ladies cover their tables, overload their mantelpieces, and weigh down their *étagères*, but everywhere comfort and an elegant simplicity. At Madame Tegner's it was easily to be seen that this room was the sanctuary of intimate home-life. It was there that you found your favorite friends and books, — books which you could read to the family, and which one loved to re-read alone. The embroidery frame, the work-box, the half-finished tapestry, and in one corner the open piano, — all proclaimed the home. On the piano were scattered loose pieces of music, many of which were the national airs, which are so popular in Sweden. The Swedish women give themselves up to domestic cares with much activity and vigilance. They love needlework no less than instructive reading; and, endowed with a most happy aptitude, they soon acquire a relative superiority in the fine arts. Marius soon perceived this, and he wondered that he had known so little of the customs of these fair women of the North-land.

The twilight shadows fell, and the lamps were brought in, the windows draped with long heavy curtains which fell to the floor, shutting out the uncertain light which prevailed at that hour, and which is all the darkness — if it can be called darkness — which they have in Sweden at this season of the year. Tegner seated himself in a vast arm-chair, and the three women sat near the table sewing. The artist approached a small stand on which were several French novels and illustrated journals from all parts of the world; he tried to read, or rather he looked at the pictures, while the ladies worked and Monsieur Tegner twirled his thumbs.

These quiet hours passed in the bosom of the family in peacefulness, embellished by all the charming sociability, and by the graces for which the Swedish women are particularly noted, and which renders Sweden so dear to foreigners, seemed delightful to this child of the South. It was a great contrast to the brilliant and animated outdoor life of Provence. Marius felt himself living in a more serene atmosphere than he had yet known. Madame Tegner herself — stiff, awkward, and constrained before the world — here found herself in her natural element. She harmonized well with the objects which surrounded her. She was a woman of the North, severe but good, reserved to strangers, and profoundly devoted to her family; and was on close acquaintance always loved by those who had at first feared her. Elfrida worked with great attention a complicated piece of tapestry, which, however, did not prevent her listening to the young Frenchman's accounts of his travels, and of French life. The merchant, fatigued by his long day of business, and determined not to impair his digestion by troublesome thoughts, forgot when he entered the drawing-room all business cares. He was seated in his enormous arm-chair, which seemed made expressly to accommodate his *embonpoint*, his hands crossed before him over his capacious waistcoat, saying nothing, thinking nothing, and enjoying a satisfactory feeling of well-being and of vegetable life.

A little aside, deftly handling two large netting-needles, her long slender hands plunged in the brown wool, her head bent, sat Carine, working near a little table by the light of a solar lamp, which enveloped her person in a sort of aureola. Marius regarded her with restrained but profound emotion. In her suave beauty he found everything to satisfy his artistic taste, — the light which dazzles, the candor which charms. His gaze went from the limpid blue eyes to the soft golden-blond hair, descended from the head to the sloping shoulders, lingered at the waist, and followed the undulating lines of her beautiful figure. " O sister of Galatea ! " thought he, " how happy would he be who could animate *thee* by a kiss ! O Carine ! Oh, if life's passions have never touched thee, if those lovely eyes have never been illumined by the light of love, then wilt thou be transfigured, adorable statue, and enchant all hearts that are now desolate ! "

Monsieur Tegner addressed to the young
girl several questions, to which she replied in
monosyllables. It was apparent that he desired to break this obstinate silence, and to
draw her into the general conversation; but
she resisted, and silently refused all overtures.
In speaking to her the merchant's voice was
affectionate and tender; it was evident that his
regard for this maiden was mixed with pity. It
was the same also with Madame Tegner and
Elfrida. Marius observed everything, and with
his usual tact refrained from any attempt to
pay Carine those ordinary attentions which are
customary between young persons of opposite
sexes in company, for he saw that she was timid
as a hind in the deep forest.

One of the guests of the preceding evening,
the red-haired Frederick Brask, came at nine
o'clock to pay a visit to Tegner. His coming
brought a little diversion and activity into this
home party, which had begun to languish and
imperceptibly feel the effect of the cloud

which Carine's melancholy threw over them.
Elfrida, seeing Frederick enter, blushed slightly
and made a joyful movement, which did not
escape the artist; she gave him her hand with
a sweet smile and a good-will which rendered
her charming. "Ah," thought Marius, "these
are lovers!"

After the arrival of a new comer in a little
circle there is always a certain movement; one
profits by it to change his position; the group
disperses and re-forms at one's pleasure: this
one leaves a sofa to take an arm-chair, that one
goes to the table, another to the piano. Elfrida
rang for tea, and she made it in the broad
window-seat, a little aside with Brask, who
seemed perfectly restored to good-humor.
Marius arose, spoke a few words to Madame
Tegner, then seated himself near the little table
where Carine worked: then he sharpened a
pencil, took a piece of Bristol board, and began
to draw. The young girl did not at first seem
to notice what he was doing, and continued

her monotonous task with her usual apathetic
indifference to everything. At last she noticed
the steadiness with which the stranger regarded
her. Marius drew with an unequalled ardor
and rapidity; he had rarely felt more rapture
and transport; a living image seemed to be
created from his fingers. But from time to
time he raised his eyes and fixed them on
Carine in a manner which was naturally em-
barrassing to her. She seldom raised her eyes;
once or twice however their eyes met, and finding those of the stranger so ardent, tenacious,
and magnetic, she quickly dropped her eyelids;
and if she felt under this magnetic glance a
new emotion, she did not permit it to be seen,
for not a muscle trembled on her impassable
visage. In the mean time the work advanced;
already the outline of the delicately modelled
forehead appeared on the paper; already one
could divine the living expression under the
long lashes, and the elegant oval (a little thin
perhaps) of the face was modelled in all its
classic purity.

The worthy host, impatient because the tea was not yet served, arose and walked up and down the room. He drew near the artist. Elfrida and Frederick came too, and grouped around him. Marius and Carine were in the centre of a little curious group. The latter endured with impatience the prolonged attention of which she was the object, and wished to leave the room ; but she could not. She therefore remained immovable and silent; but her hands trembled, and spoke for her by feverishly fingering the long box-wood needles with red sealing-wax heads, which moved only by fits and starts.

Chapter VIII.

"Good heavens! what a resemblance!" cried Tegner, "it is really striking!"

"Yes," said Brask, "it would be impossible to make a better portrait. It is Carine herself! it is Carine!"

"Do you think she is as pretty as the picture?" said Elfrida, in a low voice to the young banker.

"Oh, it is Carine!" replied he, with more frankness than gallantry.

"Yes, it *is* like her," admitted Elfrida, whose natural goodness overcame a little jealousy.

Ulrica and Gustavus now entered with the tea-trays, and the little circle was broken, much to Carine's satisfaction, who disliked to attract attention, and preferred always to remain in the background. She did not rise, but leaned toward the table; at the same time Marius held his drawing up to the light in order to criticise it. The original and the copy thus confronted each other. Carine, who had taken no notice of the picture before, recognized her own likeness, and was struck with surprise, which she betrayed by a quick gesture of her hands. She opened her mouth as if to exclaim, but suppressed the desire; then she looked again at the drawing, and at the artist who had drawn it so skilfully, so promptly, and successfully. Her face expressed her astonishment, and also perhaps a little grateful recognition for that which he had done so admirably. Her eyes glistened, as if tears arising from her heart had suddenly moistened the eyeballs; a pinkish hue tinted her cheeks, delicate and pale like the leaf of a white rose, and a light and fugitive smile deepened imperceptibly the two charming little dimples in her cheeks. All this, however, was over in an instant; she drew herself up, the smile disappeared, she became as cold as marble. Again she was a statue maiden, impassable and gloomy.

Our hero at least now knew that there was a woman within this statue, and that perhaps he might find there a heart which would respond to the palpitations of his own; but he fully realized that he must proceed cautiously, and that it is at all times necessary to deal tenderly with such delicate nervous organizations. He finished with a few strokes of his pencil the picture, which he only considered a sketch; then he threw it carelessly on the table to show Carine that he did not consider it of much importance. He then went to receive a cup of tea from Elfrida, who was doing the honors with her accustomed grace; but he could not refrain from casting sly glances at the lovely creature who always kept in the background. In a few moments, when all seemed occupied, — Elfrida with Brask, Tegner with a plate of salad, and his wife with her prayer-book, in which each evening she read the psalter for the day, — Marius, encouraged by circumstances which seemed favorable, took up his sketch and approached Carine.

"What do you think of my work?" said he.

The maiden seemed a little troubled by this unexpected question; but she replied quickly, without raising her eyes, "I think you have wasted your time. People do not take portraits of the dead!"

I do not know which impressed Marius the most, — this despairing reply, or the sound of Carine's voice. This voice was of a strange *timbre;* it had the immaterial purity of crystal, and resounded like the ideal note of a harmonica; it seemed suited to the angelic beauty of her face, for human passions could never trouble it.

Now that Marius had broken through the first barrier of reserve, — and with many women

that is always the most difficult thing to do, — he did not dream of abandoning the siege so soon. "It seems to me," said he, softly, "that you are not as dead as you think you are!"

"I am," replied Carine. "I am a hundred times more dead than those who sleep out there under the lindens." She alluded to the beautiful trees that threw their shadows, their murmurings, and their perfume over the graves in the cemetery of Gothenburg.

"Happy, then," continued the artist, "will be the one who can make you hear the trumpet of the archangel, and say to you, taking your hand, 'Carine, arise from the dead!'"

Unconsciously Marius had made the gesture which would naturally accompany such words; and if he had not blown the trumpet, his hand had at least sought that of Carine. But she had hastily drawn hers away, as if the contact had been for her a fault or a profanity, and replied, "The archangel will not sound the trumpet for or summon me, until the day of judgment."

Marius was now extremely agitated; his eyes flashed, and a light of enthusiasm illumined his brow. He had never experienced such feelings before; and doubtless he affected also the beautiful Swede, for she seemed frightened, not daring to look at this impetuous youth again, nor to speak to him. She devoted her attention closer than ever to her work, and her face became as usual cold and expressionless, and the gulf between them seemed deeper than before.

The different time-pieces struck ten. Tegner arose, and with characteristic punctuality gave the signal to retire by shaking hands with Frederick Brask and Marius Danglade; then he turned down the lamps, and pulled back the curtains. The twilight entered and filled the apartment with misty shadows. Brask, who was serene, having been restored to his usual good-humor by his long *tête-à-tête* with Elfrida, took leave of the young Frenchman with a politeness almost affectionate; and after many good wishes, each one retired.

Marius, once more in his room, went to the balcony and eagerly looked into the garden below; but the lovely vision of the preceding night did not appear. That vision seemed like a dream ; and the remembrance of her face, so noble and so pure, so virginal and chaste, came over him, and he felt sure that a thought of evil could not exist before the light of her eyes. All his suspicions had vanished, and in their place remained the tenderest sympathy.

Chapter IX.

THE days passed quietly by. One day resembled another, and nothing important occurred in the household of mine host Tegner.

Our hero was feeling completely at home, and as if he was one of the family. The austere hostess, finding him to be an honorable young man, of good habits and respectful manners, began by tolerating him, and ended

by really feeling for him a warm friendship.
Tegner treated him like a son. Elfrida be-
haved toward him as if he was her brother,
since she saw that he had no intention of making love to her. For this amiable girl was sincerity itself; she loved Frederick Brask, and
did not possess a shadow of real coquetry.

As for Carine, she was always the same.
This beautiful creature, endowed with such
unusual attractions, so well calculated to love,
so worthy of being loved, seemed to live in a
dream, and to be indifferent to everything.
She often remained for days in her room, and
on certain days it seemed as if she redoubled
her sadness. Her manner toward Marius was
also odd; sometimes she seemed attracted
toward him, and took a real interest in his
conversation. It is true she never looked at
him; but when he talked, a certain animation
was visible, and she was surprised to find herself listening with a sentiment which resembled
pleasure. After having allowed herself this

temporary relief from a mourning which she
had no doubt sworn should be eternal, she fell
into a melancholy more profound than ever.
But at least there was one pleasant result, —
the family no longer remarked those strange
changes of humor which had before been so
marked and so disturbing. The clouds were
lifting a little; she was still sad but not des·
pairing; she did not talk, but she listened;
and it was no longer forbidden for others to
address her. Slowly and almost imperceptibly
she improved; and her friends dared hope one
day to see her enter into their common life,
and interest herself once more in the things of
this world.

Marius alone could not see this improvement,
perhaps because he had not known her so long
as the others, and was also too impatient.
From the first time he had seen her, he had
felt for the lovely unfortunate a profound interest; soon that interest was changed to tenderness; little by little, without being conscious of

the change, the tenderness had become love,
and the love a profound passion, — more intense, perhaps, because hopeless. It seemed
to him that a bottomless gulf separated Carine
from the love of any man. He understood all
this; but instead of turning him from his purpose, this almost unsurmountable difficulty only
made him more determined to vanquish all
obstacles, and overcome fate itself. Very soon
this passion, which seemed to grow rapidly,
took such possession of him that he became
melancholy and almost ill. He would have
given half his life to penetrate with a ray of
light this soul, so closed and so obscure; and
seeing that he could not, his heart was wounded
sorely. Like the wounded stag, he fled to the
forest depths; he explored the beautiful country that surrounded the city; he was always on
the mountains or in the valleys; he often left
the house before daybreak, under pretext of
interesting explorations of the magnificent
country, or of curious studies, and did not

return until late at night. On those days he saw no one ; but he carried with him everywhere the dear image, which peopled for him the solitude. When he was thus far from men, far from her, he, if possible, loved her better ; then he spoke to her and she replied to him,

and he carried on imaginary conversations, and every day found himself more deeply in love. The solitude at such times was restful, and he was content. At other times, on the contrary, he felt an imperious desire to return to the family life, to see Carine oftener, and to speak with her if possible.

Chapter X.

SWEDISH hospitality, which gives without thought of return, and which restricts no one's liberty, permitted our hero to follow his own fancies, without notice or comment. In this second crisis of his life, he did not go out so much, but under pretext of work remained almost constantly in his room, hearing the many noises which were around him, and which his ear, owing to his nervous state, could distinguish with startling correctness, though vague and uncertain for others. He had learned to

distinguish Carine's lightest footstep. Often
before dawn he carried his easel into the garden, under the fallacious excuse of studying the
trunks of the fir-trees so as to paint the bark
well, but in reality to catch distant glimpses of
Carine's dress floating between the trees, as she
took her early matinal walk.

The house of Monsieur Tegner was truly a
pretty villa on the hillside, somewhat like those
châlets which give such a picturesque appearance to the country around Brisgau and to the
Oberland; but to Marius its principal charm
consisted in the presence of the golden-haired
maiden called Carine. This villa had on the
second floor a projecting window which was
beautifully carved. The architect, or builder,
who placed it there was a true artist; he had
displayed much originality in the carving, which
was in the arabesque or oriental style of
Damascus or Cairo, of which the Swedes and
Norwegians are very fond. A little balcony
surrounded this window, which was at the same

time both elegant and rustic. Over the window was a sort of projecting roof, which formed a tower, covered with a dome; and all along the dome and spire climbed a profusion of flowering creepers, — sweet-scented jasmine, and hop-vines, accompanied by a light squadron of wall-flowers, climbing rapidly, as if to take by storm on their aerial route all the other flowers and leaves. But that which Marius valued about all this was that one day on the railing of this balcony he had seen Carine leaning, to look into the garden; another time he had seen her lovely blond head peep out of the thick vines, when she had mechanically broken off some flowers of clematis and plucked dreamingly some silver stars of the fragrant jasmine. From that time this balcony was sacred to our hero! He made a masterly drawing of it, which only needed her presence to be perfect; but the window was a picture in itself. The simple merchant was astonished that his young guest took such an interest in

8

that window and balcony; but he finally attributed it to the vagaries of an artist; and he considered all artists a little queer. It was a constant source of trouble to the honest Tegner to comprehend the attraction which made a young man with such brilliant prospects prefer *art* to *trade;* so he set all his little eccentricities down to the same score, and thought that perhaps age would bring reason; and in the mean while he formed a veritable attachment for Marius, and loved him as a son.

At the hours of family reunion Marius was always the first at the rendezvous. Tegner was much surprised to find him before himself in the drawing-room, and pointed his young friend out as a model to Elfrida, who had perhaps a ribbon to tie or a pin to put in, and was usually a little late. Our hero's chief happiness was to see Carine enter the room, with her light graceful carriage, her figure at the same time elegant and frail, her lovely blond head bent shyly down. She never even looked at Marius, but he could look at her; and at table he was at her side, and it was a pleasure to render her the many little services by which well-bred men can show women their deference and respectful attention. At first she received these attentions with apparent indifference, but ended by becoming accustomed to them.

Etiquette was less severe here in Tegner's house than at the court of the petty German princes. Each guest did not have behind his chair a valet in black cloth to anticipate his wishes and satisfy his desires; one had there the right and the duty to occupy himself with his neighbor. Carine handed his glass to Marius, and he in turn took the basket and offered her the bread, passed her the fruit and asked her for the cream and sugar. Therefore there was between them a continual interchange of courtesies. Carine thanked Marius sometimes by a word and sometimes by a smile. He was indeed the light of the company. He

well knew how to make himself interesting, —
sometimes gay, and sometimes even a little buf-
foonish : the southern temperament is welcome
everywhere. The beautiful *mélancolie* took no
part in the conversation, but she listened.
Sometimes Marius turned to her suddenly, and
his eyes said, "It is for you I talk!" But
instead of flattering her these attentions dis-
turbed Carine ; she immediately became dis-
contented, formal, and abstracted ; she seemed
by her cold glance to say, "Do you not know
that I am dead to the world?" Under such a
glance Marius felt a certain bitterness ; he realized that his hopes had soared too high, only to
fall heavily to the earth.

At times also Carine did not come to her
meals for days, and Marius did not even hear
her name mentioned. These were bad days
for him ; but there were greater trials in store
for him. He had now been Monsieur Tegner's
guest over three weeks, and believed that he
had somewhat influenced this young girl ; that

he had in a measure overcome her shyness
and softened her bitter moods, — when all at
once he perceived to his great sorrow a sad
change come over her. For several days she
had appeared more calm, more interested in all
around her, as if she was gliding imperceptibly
from her melancholy and returning to ordinary
life. Physically she was expanding; her eyes
were brighter, her complexion more rosy; she
was no longer an invalid, and her friends smiled
hopefully on regarding her. It was then that
she had a relapse a hundred times worse than
the first. She enveloped herself with a coldness and reserve greater than ever before.
Formerly toward Marius she was simply apathetic; for her he did not exist. At present it
was much worse; she appeared to have an
aversion for him which was almost hatred; she
carefully avoided meeting him, and fled from
his presence; she shunned the garden because
he went there; and if at times she went to her
meals, she arrived late and left early, without

speaking a word to any one. Marius did not complain; but he thought her unjust in her caprices, and mentally accused her of all his sufferings.

Nevertheless (who can sound the depths of a feminine heart?), once or twice, turning suddenly, he found Carine looking at him intently; and moreover the expression in her eyes was not hatred. Another day Marius was reading under the shade of the large trees beside the fountain near the porphyry vase; it was a volume of Carlen's poems, which described in beautiful language the secret bitterness and the deceitful sweetness of love. He let the book fall, and raised his eyes to heaven; but on the way he looked into Carine's window. His glance did not go farther, for behind the curtain he saw a little white hand holding the muslin apart. The hand was withdrawn quickly and the drapery fell, — but not so promptly as to prevent his recognizing Carine ! This so agitated our hero that he arose suddenly and went for a long walk in the country, through an extended avenue of lindens and beeches which led to the foot of the mountains; there he thought over his acquaintance with this strange but adorable creature, and even dared to hope for the future!

"Strange girl!" murmured he as he walked rapidly on, beating with his cane the undergrowth of vines and grasses that grew so thickly in the borders of his path. "Oh, shall I ever penetrate the mysteries of her heart?"

This mystery was one of Carine's strongest attractions for Marius, and was no doubt the very thing which had enchained him. To this careless son of the South, accustomed to an easy artistic life, everything with him so far had been *couleur de rose;* he had yet to learn that often the heart of man is revealed to himself by suffering. He was aware that his love was more than he could endure; he sought everywhere the remedy, but found it not. It was impossible to appeal to Carine;

he well knew that she would not listen to him for a moment. Elfrida was too young and gay for a confidante; he was afraid she would laugh at his woes. There was nothing about Madame Tegner to inspire confidence in regard to love affairs. There remained only his host; undoubtedly Monsieur Tegner was the best of the family for that purpose. Two or three times the young man tried to speak on this subject to the worthy man. At first he began by asking some questions about Carine; but at the first word poor Tegner looked so embarrassed and troubled that from sheer pity Marius could not continue the subject, nor demand answer to his question.

Chapter XI.

YET our hero well knew that this tense state of affairs could not continue, and that a *dénouement* was imminent. He grew thin and nervous; and avowed that he was no longer himself; he certainly felt that he no longer rendered himself as agreeable to his host as politeness demanded. Like Carine, he needed solitude. He therefore resolved to leave, at least for a time, this hospitable house, and to set out immediately on a voyage to the great lakes and immense forests of the North, which he had intended to visit in the autumn.

One morning, then, Marius brusquely announced his intention to his host at breakfast,
just as they had finished their meal. No doubt
Carine was dreamily absorbed in her own
thoughts, for at that moment she let fall to
the floor, instead of putting on the table, the
glass from which she was drinking.

" What ! you are going already? " cried
Tegner, putting his hand on the young man's
arm.

" Yes," replied Marius ; " but I will return,"
added he, looking at Carine. She had resumed
her mask, and her face expressed nothing.

" And when do you go? " asked Tegner.

" To-morrow.'

" Is n't this very sudden? "

" I can wait no longer."

" And you go — "

" To the North."

" By what route? "

" By the Götha Canal."

" Impossible ! all the places are taken."

" Mine is reserved."

" Why, you *are* a careful young man."

" It is necessary in travelling."

" Well, the captain is one of my best friends. I will recommend you to him with great pleasure, if you will permit me ; but this abrupt departure seems odd to me."

"Do not suspect me of ingratitude, my dear friend ! " cried the young Frenchman, taking in his both of the merchant's hands and pressing them affectionately, ' but introduce me to your friend as soon as possible."

The remainder of the day was passed in the nervous occupations and the little preparations which always accompany a departure. Tegner, his wife, and Elfrida did everything they could to insure their guest's comfort on his journey ; they took as much interest as if he had been really their child and brother. They loaded him with as many provisions and other articles as if he were undertaking a voyage to the north pole. Marius was overwhelmed and touched by these delicate attentions; he had never seen such goodness and generosity united with such frank and unaffected cordiality.

Carine remained shut up in her room, and he was obliged to depart without seeing her.

Chapter XII.

THE vessels that run between the North and the Baltic Seas by the Götha Canal leave the port of Gothenburg at three o'clock in the morning. Therefore most of the passengers go on board the preceding evening. Marius, therefore, left the dear mansion where he had been so hospitably received, after tea, accompanied by Karl Johan and Brask, — the latter having come to pass this last evening with the young Frenchman, whom he now loved like a brother. Standing erect and solemn on the threshold like a sibyl, Brigette Tegner deigned to wish him "a happy voyage and a safe return;" and Elfrida, giving him her hand, said in a sweet voice (but looking at Brask), "Do not forget us, Monsieur, and return soon." And Marius, without doubt willing to pique his jealous friend, kissed the pretty hand held out to him, with all the grace of a gentleman of the court of Louis XV., and then with a rapid step joined his worthy host, who had already started in the direction of the port; but on arriving at the corner of the street he turned to take a last view of the place where life had suddenly taken on for him an intensity so profound. He looked earnestly at the roof which sheltered Carine, then dashing a tear from his eye and sighing deeply, he hastily rejoined his companions.

The three friends soon reached the quay where were stationed the little packet-boats that run on the Götha Canal. The captain, standing on the bridge, overlooked the loading

of merchandise and the arrival of the passengers. Seeing his old friend Tegner, he
descended to meet him and to make the
acquaintance of the young Frenchman whom
Karl Johan warmly recommended to his care.
The captain received our hero with great courtesy, and immediately installed him in one of
the best cabins near his own. Now that he
was convinced that his young friend was well
cared for, Karl Johan remembered that it was
his hour for retiring; so wishing Marius
" good-night " and *bon voyage*, he took Frederick's arm and went on shore, where, after
waving his handkerchief to his late guest, he
wended his way homeward.

Left to himself, Marius, son of a ship-owner,
naturally inspected the boat to which he had
intrusted his life. He also glanced at his
fellow travellers, condemned like himself to a
forced intimacy between these narrow planks;
then he went to the forward part of the deck
and seated himself on a bundle of ropes, and

idly listened to the songs of the sailors as they worked in the rigging. At the same time he reviewed the events of the past weeks once more. It seemed incredible to him that in so short a time more had happened to him than in his whole previous life.

Chapter XIII.

THE English are justly proud of the beautiful Caledonian Canal between Oban and Inverness, connecting the Irish and the North Seas, and which they call with their usual emphasis "Neptune's Staircase," no doubt because its liquid steps raise like mere playthings the heavy vessels of Victoria, which pass with sails set and at full steam through this artificial roadway to traverse the pine forests of Glen Nevis. It is a great work, no doubt; but one admires it less when he has seen the Canal of Götha, between Gothenburg and Stockholm.

9

This immense work is the actual result of labor, and is really one of the most brilliant miracles of force and human patience. It is difficult to realize the money and labor it has cost to cut this great canal from one sea to another; to force through forests and mountains a stream of water forty leagues long. Here following the level of torrents and lakes, there on the contrary digging through granite beds and rocks of porphyry, it is achieved by a vast system of bridges, gates, dams, basins, and aqueducts, which vanquish all the obstacles and wash the highest hills with salt sea waves. And this beautiful canal runs through such a charming and picturesque country, filled with so much historical interest; here one can recall all the pomps of history and all the enchantments of poetry. As one passes through the beautiful country filled with noble ruins, and the marvels of legendary lore unroll, mixed with the splendors of Nature, one must acknowledge that the Rhine itself, with its *cor-*

tege of feudal castles and ruined turrets, — even
the old German Rhine, — is vanquished.

September was near at hand : daylight no
longer reigned supreme, **and** there was already
a little darkness, though of very short duration ;

and toward three a band of satin lightened
the horizon, and announced once more the daybreak. The bell sounded its last call, the chain
which fastened the boat to the wharf was taken
in, and above the masts and ropes puffed and
streamed the waves of black smoke ; then the
heavy mass shook, the water became agitated

and foamy, the paddle wheel revolved, and the
"Edda" confided herself to the waves of the
river Götha, and struggled bravely against
the current.

Seated on a pile of ropes near the sailor who
held the tiller, insensible to the beauties of the
landscape which unrolled before him, Marius
followed eagerly with his eyes the fading view
of Gothenburg, which grew fainter each moment, and soon almost disappeared on the
horizon. At last a bend in the river and a
small hill concealed even this distant view.
Our hero's heart sunk within him; but he soon
rallied, and said to himself, "Be a man! Am
I a weak child that I should give way like
this?" He arose, and going to the bow of the
boat mingled with the busy group of passengers,
who looked admiringly on the beautiful scenery
through which they were passing. To the fertile plains that surrounded the city already succeeded the most wild and abrupt scenes. The
vessel glided swiftly by steep hills bristling with

great rocks of grotesque forms, covered with moss, lichens, and heather, above which enormous pine-trees stood like superb odalisques of verdure. In any other mood the young artist would have been enchanted with such grand scenery (now smiling, now terrible) incessantly offered to his regard; but when one suffers, it is the heart and not the sky which must change. Nevertheless, he took his sketch-book and his pencils, and anxious to forget himself in labor he tried to draw rapidly, in passing, the marvels of Nature by which he was surrounded.

Toward evening the "Edda" entered at full steam the waters of Wener, a lake large as a sea. The atmosphere was transparent and serene; the water was like a vast crystal mirror, —smooth as glass. In the wake of the steamer lay a long track of silver, with occasionally light flakes of foam. All Nature was calm, quiet, and peaceful. Marius gazed dreamily at this silver pathway; the soft light of Aurora threw upon it the prismatic colors, which lighted with

unearthly radiance, and like the velvet lining of
a jewel-casket, the little rainbow-colored drops
— diamonds, sapphires, emeralds, and liquid
rubies — that sparkled and scintillated. · In the
distance appeared the lofty mountain of Kinne-
kulle, which is called the " Crown of Sweden,"
— like to an immense wave which in time of
tempest had risen up from the depths of Lake
Wener, and which the wand of a magician had
suddenly struck with an eternal immobility.
On its sides Nature has lavished her richest
treasures. Forests spread over it; meadows
with luxuriant verdure bloomed upon it, en-
amelled with thousands of wild flowers; lovely
gardens smiled near flourishing orchards, —
everywhere were beauty and verdure, and the
pretty cottages on the hillside were surrounded
by well kept lawns. Here and there little vil-
lages climbed on the mountain's shoulder, and
the large iron cross (the holy symbol of Chris-
tianity) which surmounted the little white or
red churches rose to heaven in the midst of

large trees. Soon the steamer passed by the
famous rock of Whalle-Hall, from the top of
which the Scandinavian warriors who had not
been so fortunate as to fall in battle precipi-
tated themselves into the lake, hoping by this
voluntary sacrifice to propitiate the gods, and

to obtain admission into their military paradise. At last, after having saluted *en passant*
the Gothic ruins (which are rare in Sweden)
of the old manor of Lecko, and the pleasant
village of Bruneby, which seems to burst out
of the bosom of verdure, the " Edda" stopped
in front of the convent of Wreta-Kloster.

The captain, who had been busily occupied

conducting his vessel safely through the lake,
had not yet had time to pay Marius any attention, as he had promised his friend Tegner he
would do. But arrived at the station where
the steamer was to make a little stay, he sought
the young stranger, and claimed, with a win-
ning cordiality full of grace, the pleasure of
his company. He had already noticed the
melancholy expression of the Frenchman; and
he felt that he owed it to the honor of Sweden
to disperse, if possible, the cloud under which
the young man evidently rested, and to cause
him to carry home with him a good impression
of this northern land.

Petrus Mandel was the captain's name; he
was a distinguished officer in the Swedish navy,
and like many of his fellow officers had passed
several years in the French squadron, where
he had acquired those elegant manners and
customs which form part of the traditions of
this elegant corps. Called to a brilliant career,
Petrus, officer of fortune (that is to say, he

had *no* fortune), chanced to meet an extremely beautiful and seductive woman, with whom he fell in love. But he remembered the old stanza in the Saga: "On land make love; on the water never! On a vessel even Freya herself would deceive; it is a deceitful smile which dimples her lovely cheeks, and her floating tresses become nets to ensnare thee." Ebba was the name of his beloved, and she drew him to the shore with silken tresses. He no more took pleasure in these long voyages which separated him so cruelly from his sweetheart; a year seemed an age. So he resigned his position in the navy, and accepted the command of one of the finest steamers belonging to the canal company.

"I regret," said he to Marius, "that my duties have thus far prevented me from enjoying your society. It would have given me great pleasure to point out to you the beauties of our lakes and torrents; but one cannot always do as one wishes: I am a proof of this saying. But at present, at least, I am at liberty; that is to say, I am at your service."

Marius was in such a melancholy mood that perhaps he would have preferred solitude to even the excellent company of the good captain; but the offer was made with such frank cordiality, that it was not possible to refuse. The captain took his new friend's arm, and while the other passengers went on shore and installed themselves in a shabby-looking inn, he conducted our hero to supper in his private salon.

There is nothing like full glasses — when one has emptied them — to establish confidence. At the end of an hour Danglade and Mandel were like old friends; they had already discussed many subjects, and found that they agreed very well. Between two men both young and both men of the world there is usually a certain sympathy; and with elbows on the table they talked and laughed with the abandon which one always finds at the bottom of the third bottle of good Rhine wine. Love in its thousand varieties, the sentiment under many aspects, — the fidelity of some, the hypocrisy of others, — was analyzed and discussed gravely, with a calmness of words and a brightness of observation which would have done credit to two philosophers. But for intelligence of *affaires du cœur* find me two philosophers equal to two lovers!

This conversation completely changed the course of Danglade's ideas, for he had passed the day in a sort of dreamy stupor.

The captain, delighted with the effect he had produced, wishing to profit by the leisure he now enjoyed (for the steamer had a number of locks to pass through), proposed a visit to the beautiful ruins of the ancient convent of Wreta-Kloster. The evening was superb, the air pure and bracing, the sky serene and un-troubled. In a *cortége* of purple and gold clouds the sun descended slowly toward the mountains of Norway; the pine-trees which fringed the borders of the lake exhaled their pungent and balmy odor on the air; the heath-cocks flew about overhead, sending forth hoarse and shrill cries; little squirrels hopped from branch to branch, peering at the strangers curiously but fearlessly with their bright eyes, then bounding lightly from tree to tree; the oblique rays of the setting sun threw a rosy light on the water, and all Nature was beautiful, fresh, and serene.

The young men walked slowly for some time in silence amid the vast ruins made by the hand of man, but which kind Nature had already partly covered with a verdant mantle of ivy and saxifrage. In the midst of these broken columns, these inverted arches, these prostrate pillars; in face of this cloister, dead itself, and which only interested by its death, — they arrived at the entrance of a vast cemetery covered with tombs, some fallen, others still standing, but all covered with inscriptions. The people of the North are known to excel in this literature of the tomb. Death always inspires them with pious thoughts, often profound; but it has for them no fear or terror, and they always greet it as a kind friend.

The thoughts of Marius were far from being so calm; his wounds were again opened. He gradually withdrew from his companion and began to dream again; but the captain, who did not wish to leave him alone, soon joined him, and surprised him in the act of reading earnestly this epitaph, engraved on the tomb of a young man, —

> "King, behold thy destiny!
> Slave, behold thy release!
> Beauty, behold these bones!
> Savant, behold this empty skull!
> Rich man, behold this dust!
> Pauper, behold this world!"

"Very good," said Petrus; "see him fallen into melancholy again. Attention!" and then, following a manœuvre familiar to great tacticians, he made what is called a "diversion."

"Come," said he, "I wish to show you one of the most beautiful views in Sweden."

Then drawing Marius away from the tomb, the captain led him through a serpentine path, and soon arrived at a large rock, which formed a natural platform in the midst of the most luxuriant vegetation. Here were trees and shrubs of all colors and varieties, and spread out like a vast panorama before them was a magnificent scene. There were the two lakes, the winding canal which united them, a range of hills rising one above the other like the steps of a gigantic ampitheatre, and still farther off, in the extreme distance, a waving girdle of large trees.

"Behold Sweden! Is it not beautiful?" asked the captain, touching the young man's shoulder good-naturedly.

"Magnificent!" replied he ; then, stretching his arm toward the southwest, "Is not Gothenburg there?" asked he, not without blushing a little.

"Yes," replied Mandel, looking at him roguishly; "Gothenburg is there — and Carine also!"

At the sound of the name so ever present to his thoughts, Marius blushed deeply; then grew suddenly pale. "Ah," said he in a few moments, without looking at Mandel, "you know Carine?"

"Yes," said the captain; "and I am, perhaps, of all her friends, he who best knows the secrets of her sad young life."

Marius was silent; but his trembling lips and fixed look spoke for him. His very silence was as eloquent as a prayer, and seemed to say to the young officer, "Speak! I implore you!"

"Have you heard nothing of her history from Tegner?" asked the captain at last.

"Absolutely nothing. I have not even dared to ask her father."

"She is not Tegner's daughter."

"Who is she, then?"

" His niece."

" Is she an orphan? "

"No ; but she is unfortunate. When Tegner (who is goodness itself) heard of the event which had almost unsettled her reason and compromised her life, . . . the good man proposed to his sister, the mother of Carine (who lives in the country), to send her daughter to Gothenburg to him, so that she might be diverted by the distractions of city life."

" He has succeeded well ! " murmured Marius.

"That is not his fault ; it is rather Carine's, for she will not be consoled."

"What has she lost, then?"

"That is a long story," replied the captain, "and it would take a long while to relate it to you."

" But the hours are long, and we have nothing to do," said Marius, leaning his elbow on his knee and resting his head upon his hand, in the attitude of one who wishes to listen attentively and without losing a word of the story.

"Carine is not a native of Gothenburg," said Mandel; "she was born some distance

from that city, in a little village that we passed this morning on our way."

"What! and you did not tell me?" cried the young man, interrupting him.

"Eh? How did I know that it would interest you, I should like to know?"

"You are right," replied Marius, hanging his head, "pardon me. I know you will, won't you?"

"Certainly, my friend," said the good captain, laughing; "we never expect reason from a lover, eh?"

Marius did not reply, but continued the subject: "You say that we passed her native village?"

"Yes; it is called Lilla-Edet, and is situated a few miles from the cascades of Trolhätta, which you did not care to visit."

"What did she do? Why has she left her home? Why is she now in Gothenburg? And above all, why is she so — so sad?"

"But you demand the whole history in a word!"

"Yes, without doubt. I wish to hear all."

"Listen, then," said the captain. "Carine is the daughter of Monsieur Tegner's sister; her family is not wealthy, but they are in comfortable circumstances, and highly respectable. She has an unusual sense of honor, and has received an excellent education. I do not know how old you think she is, but she is just nineteen, although she does not appear to be more than sixteen; but misfortune has already pressed heavily on this poor girl."

"What, then, has happened to her?" cried Marius; "really, you frighten me!"

The captain did not reply directly, but continued: "With her father and her mother she lived peacefully and happily, honored and respected. She is very beautiful; but I need not tell *you* that, — you have seen her."

Marius made an affirmative sign, and sighed.

"Unfortunately," continued the captain, "the son of a rich neighboring farmer, who had been educated in Stockholm, returned to establish himself in the neighborhood. I can only tell you that he was a phœnix. Carine was nearly eighteen, admired and courted by all the rustic beaux of the vicinity; she had never loved, and she had arrived at that age when young people are most susceptible. Olaf was the young man's name; he soon paid her marked attention, and sought not to deceive her.

Carine had been raised too chastely for him to hope to persuade her against honor. He respected her, and contented himself with being honest, and spoke of marriage."

"And she listened to him?" cried Marius.

The captain not heeding this question went on with his story: "The more chaste a maiden is the better she knows how to love. She had never before listened to words of love; her heart was as virgin as that of Mother Eve the day when, taking her by the hand, God gave her as a wife to the first man. But more faithful than Eve, this lovely blonde did not listen to the serpent. In a word, she loved with all her heart."

Mandel could see by the expression of his young friend's face that it was very bitter for him to hear that Carine had loved another man, and he hastened to say: "She was wrong, and will some day realize it; very few men are worthy of such love." Then he again resumed the story: —

"Carine's parents, wise and prudent, did not view the prospect of this union with enthusiasm. They loved their daughter, and Olaf did not seem to them likely to be a husband who would make his wife happy. But what reply could they make to their beloved daughter, who came to them so confidingly, and embracing them said, 'I love and I am loved!' Could they say, 'Bless you child,' and rejoice with her? It was Olaf's father who solved the problem. Where his son had the merit of seeing only a question of sentiment, *he* saw a question of ciphers. He weighed Carine's *dot*, and found it too light compared with that of his son; it lacked some hundreds of rix-dollars before the 'Pearl of Sweden' (as Carine was called) would be worthy of this peasant, who had been refined in the schools.

"To do Olaf justice, he was very sorry that his father should be so determined against the marriage; for he loved the maiden as much as he was capable of loving, and that perhaps is not saying much. But he did not possess enough force of character to combat his father's will. 'We will wait,' said he to Carine. 'Wait! for what?' cried she. 'You know that I will never be any richer.' 'Life is long,' replied he, 'and my father may change.' .

"In the mean time family pride, — the consciousness of a long line of worthy ancestors and of a spotless name, — awakened in the soul of Carine's father. 'You must forget him,' said he to his daughter. 'It is impossible!' cried the poor girl. 'You can if you wish,' replied the father, who had passed the age of love; and as he believed that one love would drive away another, he made up his mind to find a husband for his child. When this was proposed to her she was in despair, and resisted with an energy of which one would not have believed her capable. Her mother called her 'disobedient.' Carine wept, but would not consent. Her father said he

would turn her out of the house. 'Very well,'
said she, 'I will go to-morrow.'

"Do not be too indignant, my young friend,"
continued the captain, perceiving the wrath of
Marius, whose fists were doubled. "Her
parents were neither wicked nor heartless; if
they tried to compel their daughter it was
because they believed it was for her happiness.
It is always the happiness of their children
that most parents desire ; only it often happens
that they take the worst means to obtain it.
But when Carine's parents realized . that they
were only making matters worse, they changed
their tactics and returned to their former tenderness and natural goodness, — at times more
tender than ever, because they wished to atone
for their seeming cruelty.

"But Carine had lost her peace of mind;
she regarded herself as an ungrateful and disobedient child, whom God would punish. She
reproached herself with this obstinate resistance to the will of her parents; and yet she

could not make up her mind to yield. First
love had taken deep root in her young soul.
With the courage she had, with this noble faith
in her beloved (which is found in the hearts
of all women who have not been deceived by
man, who have not been disenchanted), all
was possible !

"Ah, if Olaf had really been worthy of her,
if he had even had the same courage and the
same strength of character, these two loving
hearts might have conquered all, and would
have overcome every obstacle and have been
happily united.   But Olaf, — and mark that
these weak and cowardly men are too often
the heroes of a romantic passion of the best
and the most noble of women, — Olaf lacked
all the strong virtues; he did not possess
mental strength enough to take a decided
position, or to oppose a stronger will.   He
was a handsome animal, and contented himself by giving Carine the vulgar consolations
of his barren tenderness.   He believed that

if they were patient, something would happen in their favor, and that time only could aid them. He said he was very sorry that Carine's *dot* was not larger — or rather that his father did not think it enough. 'Always this question of money!' murmured the girl, a secret bitterness already arising in her heart. She finally took an heroic step. She had an aunt at Stockholm who was her mother's sister; she had no children and was well off, living very comfortably. She was very fond of her niece, and loved to have her with her. Carine asked permission to go and stay with her aunt for some time. Her parents seeing her so sad dared not refuse; they hoped that this journey would prove a distraction for her, and that she would return cured. Man is ingenious to persuade himself, and it is that which he desires that he usually believes; so her parents made all necessary preparation, and saw their daughter depart tearfully but hopefully.

"Stockholm is not as large as Paris; but

at least it is the capital of Sweden. That is enough to say that all the miseries concentrate here; that here covetousness and greed assemble; that the ambitious here fight the battle of life. What could a simple country maid, who had nothing but her innocence and her beauty, do in the midst of this crowd? Gain money? It was for that she had come! Gain money? — terrible word full of anguish, even in the mouths of strong men; a hundred times more frightful in that of a woman!

"But there was a Providence. Carine found that her aunt was very good; she received her niece with sincere affection, and forced her to busy herself. There are many dangers for a lovely young girl in a large city like Stockholm; but God permitted Carine to escape them. She-threw around herself a strange fascination, — you yourself have felt it; but at the same time she lived in such a serene atmosphere of modesty and reserve as to command respect. Her aunt took a great

interest in her, and protected her, and found
her employment. It did not promise to make
her rich rapidly, but at least it gave her a
certain independence so dear to those who
have true self-respect and dignity.

" Built on three islands, on the border of a
large bay, pierced by canals which divide it
into quarters, or sections, the city of Stockholm
has more boats than carriages; indeed it has
been called 'the Venice of the North.' Its
inhabitants, born sailors, prefer their rapid skiffs
to the *fiacres* and to the *droschkies*, which wait
at each wharf the orders of the voyagers.
Without having the grand classic shape of the
Venetian gondola or the *svelte*, or the robust
lightness of the *kaïks* of Constantinople, yet
the boats of Stockholm are charming. It is
very pleasant on the morning of a beautiful
summer day to see the squadron, with their
green-painted decks, their sterns ornamented
with leaves and flowers, dash up Skeppsbro
(*Quai de la marine*) to take on their pas-

sengers, proud of making the trip in ten minutes. These boats are entirely managed by young girls, who are usually good-looking, having graceful forms and fresh complexions. The man who would dare to interfere with their business would immediately be thrown head first into the bottom of the Baltic. The rudder falls like a distaff, and it is really a picturesque scene — like the *opera comique* — to see on deck these water-women, at the same time engaging, modest, and romantic, with their white, sleeveless, open blouses over a red bodice with red sleeves, their short green skirts reaching only to the knees, and their scarlet stockings. While the two strongest girls put in motion the ingenious machinery of the wheels, which obey their hands better than steam, the third plays on the bagpipe or sings the national songs, which last always find an echo in the depths of the Swedish heart. Most of these *batelières* are *fiancées*, too poor, alas! to marry; and they have come from

their native province to gain the modest
salary which will aid them to buy their
trousseau, whilst their patient lovers cut porphyry in the quarries of Elfsdal, or seek for
silver in the mines of Kongsberg. All these
maidens form a unique and charming class of
Swedish society, and are so strongly banded
together that they form a veritable corporation,
administered by women.

"This, then, was Carine's work. They gave
her one of the best places in the office. It
would not do to expose her delicate complexion to the ardent rays of the summer sun
or the fierce winds of the Baltic sea. Our
young heroine soon won the esteem and love
of her companions; it was impossible to resist
her sweetness and good temper. In a short
time she wore their costume; and it was
worth while to see her when she appeared in
the morning on the quay to give the orders
and instruction of the day. Fresh as the dawn
and as smiling, her cheeks no longer pale, but

colored like the wild rose ; her graceful form,
her beautiful hands, and her lovely blond
hair, — one could easily imagine they beheld
one of the immortal Valkyries who dwell in
the Scandinavian paradise of Odin.

"Carine would have been happy if regret for
the absent had not oppressed her heart. She
had written to her lover one of those adorable
letters in which a woman unveils her whole
heart ; she told him that now she was support-
ing herself, and that it was for him she was
working. 'For the rest,' added she, 'for those
who are intelligent and courageous, Stockholm
is an admirable city, where each one is sure to
find employment of his forces, the price of his
courage, and the recompense of his labors. It
is only necessary to will and to dare.' Carine
was not learned, and, God be praised ! she did
not write like an author ; but her letter was
adorable ; it was full of charming things, strong
sentiments, written admirably. On receiving
such a letter a true-hearted man would have

been willing to bound over the cataracts of Trolhätta, and swim the two lakes to throw himself at her feet."

"A true-hearted man never would have let her go!" cried Marius.

"You are right," said the captain; "but Olaf was *not* such a man. He replied by phrases more or less ambiguous; he assured her that he was happy to hear she was doing so well; that it would always be a happiness to him to have known her; that he regretted very much the position they were in; that times were hard, and it took a great deal of money to live; and that he had not yet found any way of gaining it. Many reasons and excuses, but not a trace of emotion! When she received his letter Carine felt her heart rise in her throat; but when she read it, she trembled with cold chills. Ah, it was not thus that she had written to him!

Chapter XIV.

"YET the illusion that she was truly loved soon returned to this beautiful soul, too pure to admit a thought of evil, too generous to cherish suspicion. I know not how she deceived herself, or what excuse she made for such conduct; but she soon resumed her dreams of love and hope.

"Meanwhile the rumor of her great beauty and grace and of her wisdom spread through the city, and one talked of nothing else in Stockholm but the beautiful Dalecarlian; for they attributed to her the nationality of her costume. Thank God! we do not yet put all our poetry in our books, and we are careful to keep some for our lives. All the world *faisait la cour*, as the French call it, to the charming Carine; but when they found their gallantry was wasted, and that nothing could impair this virtue, intact and brilliant as a diamond, several men of good standing — among others the son of a very wealthy banker — offered their fortunes and their name; but this girl believed that one could love but once, and would not listen to them. Then her aunt was taken sick and died, leaving her little fortune to her niece. Carine had but one thought, but one end, — to return to her home and to Olaf! Her aunt's affairs were in good shape; everything was soon settled, and she took possession of her heritage.

"Carine left Stockholm. Oh, happy voyage! although she found it very long. With what joy she watched the shining roofs, the brilliant cupolas of the capital disappear! It was the country and her province that she longed to see. With what emotion she traversed the grand lakes which separated her from her

beloved! What ineffable delight when afar off, in the midst of the lofty trees which surrounded it, she perceived the spire of the village church in which she had so often prayed, and where the priest who had instructed her from infancy would soon ask God's blessing on her union with Olaf! Yes, he was worthy of her, she

thought : she was too sincere to suspect. She
would try to return unobserved, for she wished
to give every one a surprise, and to see how
happy they would be to hear of her good fortune, and to hear each one wish her good-luck.
She avoided disembarking at the village wharf,
so as not to attract too much attention. · Soon
she found herself in the fields a little below
Lilla-Edet, and by a *detour* with which she was
familiar she hastened to her parental roof.

" But after entering the village Carine paused
a moment on the summit of a hill which commanded a view of the valley below, that she
might see the houses, the streets, and the gardens in the midst of which she had passed her
youth, — her happiest years. Suddenly she
heard a joyous chime of bells, and as their
merry peals rang out on the clear summer air
they seemed to welcome her with their light
and poetic voices : these daughters of the sky
chanted her joy ! The maiden's heart palpi-
tated as she recognized these charming voices

that were so familiar to her ear; they seemed like a distant call from her lover. She hastened her steps, and taking a short path down the hill, she ran joyously — eyes beaming, cheeks glowing like the rose — toward the village.

"The house of God is the first thing one meets on entering Lilla-Edet. Situated at the extreme limit of the parish, it seems to salute the stranger, and to promise a clement hospitality to all travellers who arrive in this beautiful valley. Carine resolved to stay a few moments in the church; hers was a devout soul, like all pure, tender natures. She wished to thank the good God for having protected her in such a wonderful manner, — the good God who had conducted her and led her. She entered. The edifice was full of people, dressed in holiday attire. A young girl was at the altar in bridal costume, with the brilliant crown of a Scandinavian virgin upon her head; the golden circle, set with pale pearls from Lapland and with brilliant island stones, adorned her tresses. 'I will pray for her happiness,' thought Carine, kneeling reverently and making the sign of the cross; 'to-day I wish every one in the world were happy!' But just as she raised her head, the bridegroom turned, so that she saw his face.

"It was Olaf!

"Carine with difficulty repressed a scream; she grew pale, and trembled, but she did not say a word. She arose, left the church, and tried to find her way home; but she was so dazed that she soon lost herself in the fields. A peasant who met her, struck with her wild looks and her Dalecarlian costume, so different from that of this province, ran to her; at the same moment, overcome with weakness, she sank fainting to the ground. Happily the peasant recognized the poor child; and bearing her in his arms, like the good shepherd caring for his wounded lambs, he carried her to her father's house.

"The sorrowful parents did not understand their daughter's malady for a long time. They questioned her, but she could not reply intelligently. Only the name of Olaf and the word 'forgotten' passed her lips, and that so quietly that nothing could be made of it. Carine had lost her reason! But, thanks be to God, it was only temporary; the divine' spark was not extinct, and its flame soon reappeared. But the poor forsaken one had fallen into melancholy, from which nothing could rouse her.

"Olaf and his young wife dwelt near Carine in the village, and their presence was intolerable to her. She often met him, sometimes alone, sometimes with his wife; but alone or with his wife, each time she met him she felt the secret wound in her heart open and bleed afresh. She did not wish to put off the Dalecarlian costume, which recalled happier days; she kept it to remind her of her wrongs. In other ways she was more tender, more helpful,

and affectionate than ever toward her parents;
she did not wish them to suffer for her sadness.
But they would not be consoled; they knew
she suffered, and they wept.   At times her
sadness was so profound that they feared she
could not survive.

"Luckily, about this time Tegner came to
Lilla-Edet. You know he is good and affectionate, and that under his egotism he is an
excellent man — after dinner.   He found his
niece very ill;   he saw that she needed a
change of scene, and he proposed a visit to
Gothenburg. Carine would have preferred to
remain at home. Without daring to own it
even to herself, it seemed to her that she would
suffer more where *he* was not; but her uncle
and her father insisted, and she yielded.
Without seeing or speaking with her false
lover she left Lilla-Edet and went with her
uncle.

"I have told you all.   The cloud which
overshadowed her reason is gone, but there

remains a profound sadness. She is indifferent to everything, flies from the world and loves solitude. At her uncle's they are wise, and never notice her peculiarities; she has perfect liberty in her actions, her words, and her silence, — you must have observed it. She goes and comes as she pleases; remains shut up in her room, or mingles with the family. Little by little they can perceive that this calm and peaceful home-atmosphere has had a salutary influence over her troubled soul. The bitter part of her sorrow is softened, and she may recover."

Chapter XV.

IT is not necessary to tell what emotions assailed the heart of the listener to this melancholy tale. Mandel spoke no more; yet Marius listened still, until the steam-whistle and the ringing of the bell were heard.

"They have passed the ninth sluice," said the captain; "it is time for us to join the boat. The portion of the canal which follows is very different, and I must take charge myself when we enter the Wetter."

Marius did not reply. He remained motionless, leaning against a rock, his head bent on
his hands, lost in profound thought.

"Come," said Mandel, touching his shoulder
lightly.

"Where? Why?" cried Marius with a wild
air.

"To Stockholm, then," replied the captain.
"The sun sets; it is true it will soon rise,"
added he, "but that is no reason why you
should pass the night on this heath. Come!"

The young artist arose and followed the
officer mechanically. He was a little like
Carine when she returned from the city and
found her lover married. He had no energy,
no will.

The night was passed on the canal. Although so short, it seemed very long to our
hero, perplexed as he was by the most cruel
thoughts which could agitate a loving heart.
But in spite of his troubles he had one consolation. Carine had been unhappy, very unhappy

without doubt, and he felt a deep pity for her;
but she had not been guilty of any wrong; and
it was happiness for him to know that which for
a loyal and true heart is everything, — to know
that he could esteem as much as he loved.
But his uncertainty was no less great; and in the
interest even of Carine he really did not know
what part to take. If he had listened to his
heart he would have returned immediately to
Gothenburg. But how could he explain to
Tegner this sudden return? How would he
justify it in Carine's eyes? Her manner toward
him had never encouraged him to be attentive
to her. Had she ever shown him anything but
coldness and indifference, even aversion? And
had he any right to console her? On the other
hand it was evident to him that Carine suffered
more than was right, and that her grief was
more in her head than her heart. At her age
there is no wound so deep that it cannot be
healed, and she would some day realize that
Olaf was unworthy. Ah, now that he knew the

secret of her sadness, how he would like to speak consoling words to her, — words which would calm her irritation and soften her regrets ! But *would* she ever listen to him ? Alas, he knew not.

Aurora already threw her silvery light over the forests, lakes, and mountains, and still Marius was wrapped in revery, as uncertain, troubled, and vague as ever. All the other passengers had retired to their cabins to sleep away the hours that in this radiant season they call night. Only our young friend remained on deck. He had not slept the previous night, and sad as he felt he could not prevent the goddess of slumber from enveloping him in her dusky mantle ; he gradually drooped, — overcome with fatigue. A sailor who passed by threw over him a pilot-cloth, and for several hours Marius forgot the world — and Carine.

When he awoke it was broad daylight, for the sun was already high in the heavens. He saw the captain by his side.

"Well, how goes it?" said the Swede, giving him his hand in hearty greeting.

"I have slept," murmured Marius, shrugging his shoulders.

"That is a good sign," said Mandel, "espe-

cially if your sleep has been dreamless. But shake your feathers and walk a little, for you have taken a very good way to get the rheumatism."

Marius arose, and threw a rapid glance around him. The "Edda," under a fresh west wind, glided lightly over the waters of Lake Wetter, which still bears the superstitions and terrors of ancient days. Here, perhaps, is one of the most beautiful scenes of a Swedish voyage. The foliage of the oaks, the birch-trees, and the elms intermingle with the pines, forming a mass of verdure which is lovely indeed, and the lofty banks have an incomparable grandeur and majesty. In face of these beautiful scenes the artist awoke in the man, and our hero could not refrain from taking a lively interest in this unrivalled display of grandeur and beauty.

Soon detonations, hollow and irregular, like the sound of distant artillery, came from the bosom of the waves. "The Undine of the Lake, the Sea Nymph, the Spirit of the Wetter," explained the captain. "She foresees the approach of a storm, and will soon fly from her palaces, her gardens, and her castles to seek in the depths of the abyss a sure refuge."

"Where then are her gardens, her palaces, and her castles?" demanded Marius, "for I have not seen them."

The air was calm, the atmosphere serene, and the sun was encircled by a girdle of vapor, which often promises a fine day. Suddenly the lake was transformed : the horizon dilated, the waves seemed to touch the clouds ; and strange phantoms, weird and marvellous, seemed to float between heaven and earth before the astonished eyes of the travellers.

Marius, who had seen the beautiful mirage which misleads the steps of the hunter in the plain *de la Crau immense*, who had seen in the Strait of Messina the wonderful phenomena of the Fata Morgana, was nevertheless struck with astonishment on perceiving in the distance these gothic castles, these impregnable fortresses, which seemed to float in the air, in the clouds, and over the mountains. He was astonished, and asked himself if in the midst of these apparitions he would not at last perceive the enchanting and lovely form of Carine? It seemed a fitting place for her in this enchanted world of fairy palaces. But while he still sought her form in this magic scene the atmosphere became troubled; the tempest descended in fury, the castles and palaces faded silently away, and the beautiful vision vanished.

The "Edda," which was elegantly built, but not strong enough to brave a tempest, approached the east shore of the lake, near the walls of the ancient city of Wadstena, where may still be found the noble ruins of a convent, founded ages ago by Saint Brigitta, who was the daughter of a king. The ruins are beautiful, and not less celebrated. Marius said he wished to stop and visit them, to seek for traces of the vanished splendor which had formerly rendered Wadstena so famous. He added that he found the vessel light, the waves heavy, and that he did not wish to continue his voyage that day.

"Well, go if you must," said Mandel, as he saw the trunk of our hero put on shore. "Go, and may God guide you! One cannot avoid destiny."

Marius had not yet decided what to do, and he walked carelessly through the town until he came to a modest inn near the ruins of the convent. Here he decided to remain, at least for the present. Reason told him it would be the height of folly to return to Gothenburg, but he did not wish to go farther away from *her.* He could see the noble ruins from his window, and spent much time musing on their former grandeur. To-day there remained very little but the abbey, besides the cell and oratory of the saint. Many times he visited the ruins, and he never crossed their threshold without feeling a profound and pious emotion. If he could not regain his calmness of mind, which seemed to have fled from him, he still sought at least to hear the mysterious murmur of that spirit which passed over him like a breath in his dreams of Saint Brigitta, declaring to him the revelation so celebrated in the Scandinavian world.

Our young friend remained five days in Wadstena. It was the season of the year in which formerly came the devout pilgrims; and in the middle ages a pilgrimage to this place ranked second only to a voyage to Rome or Palestine; but the pilgrims were godly men and women, and seldom carried to the feet of Saint Brigitta hearts troubled by earthly passions like that of Marius. At the end of five days his impatience was greater than his will; and if he still resisted his desire to join Carine, he decided at least to abbreviate the distance which separated them. He once more embarked on the "Edda," which after touching at Stockholm returned to her station at Gothenburg.

"I hoped to see you to-day," said the captain, receiving him at the top of the ladder. "You are very welcome."

The men shook hands warmly. They had both loved: this was enough to make them sympathetic.

"Do you return to Gothenburg?" asked Mandel.

"No," said Marius, shaking his head; "I do not go so far as that — yet."

"Where are you going, then?"

"I do not know yet myself, but not far from *her.*"

He passed a day on board the "Edda," and then said good-by to his friend again, at the foot of the mountains of Trolhätta.

There is not perhaps in all Sweden a landscape more austere, more grand, and at the same time more melancholy than this region of Trolhätta. In the distance a loud murmur is heard; it increases as one draws nearer, and sounds like distant thunder. Soon the mighty voice of the cataract becomes more distinct; the solitude is filled with the sound of rushing waters; nothing can yet be seen, — as yet one *hears* it only. Soon the whole mountain seems to be covered with a cloud of spouting, dashing dust; but the waterfalls still elude the sight. For a long time one must scale the highest, steepest rocks in the midst of fallen trunks of immense trees, of thorn bushes and stunted birches. At last one finds himself in face of this wonder! Over heaps of jagged rocks a river precipitates itself, furious, foaming, and tormented in its narrow bed, torn by the bristling, pointed rocks, unquiet, violent as a steed which rears and escapes in a moment of fury or fright, from a height of one hundred feet it is engulfed in the abyss below. The scene is terrible, yet beautiful! Imagine an avalanche of foam, a torrent of snow, — of liquid snow, — a dazzling hell of water! Some distance below the abyss, burying all this foam and wrath, the torrent becomes suddenly calm and limpid. After having vanquished all, it is itself vanquished. The *mise en scène* is admirably sus-

tained, and around the cataracts the forest-trees
and shrubs crown the steep banks with their
varied foliage. Here all the different species
mix and marry. The silvery willows lean over
almost into the foam of the torrent, trailing
their long weeping branches in the water; the
beeches, with their smooth, shining, and mot-
tled bark, struggle for place side by side with
the rugged oaks; nor do the graceful elms
shrink from their neighbors the stately pines.
In the bosom even of the rushing, foaming
water, where a little earth was heaped up
among the stones and pebbles, grew different
shrubs and bushes peculiar to this northern
climate, — silver poplars and the weeping ash,
whose branches and leaves scattered and floated
in the wind. Here and there even in the midst
of the torrent, in the bosom of the dashing,
tumbling waves, little verdant islets sprang up,
like the baskets of flowers that the water
nymphs of the cascade bear in their arms.
The Flora of the waters loosed her girdle over

them, their variegated banks contrasting with the severe nakedness of the grand rocks which surrounded them.

The cataracts of Trolhätta form in themselves a little world. Divided into five branches which swerve, then reunite in such a way as to resemble a double fan, they occupy a vast space on the mountain; and the artist, the poet, the unhappy lover, or the enthusiastic lover of Nature can pass there long days, nourishing his dreams, his thoughts, his desires, and his illusions. From time immemorial, in the bosom of this strange freak of nature, the weird and gigantic imagination of the North has exalted the name alone of Trolhätta, which means *Terreur des Sorciers*, the name indicating the rôle that the marvellous plays in its history. The Norse legends of this region tell us of miracles and enchantments more or less terrible; of lovely princesses carried off by sorcerers; of murdered travellers; of mischievous dwarfs; of knightly heroes seeking

their assistance to deliver some fair lady im-
prisoned by a stern father; of giants who
thought nothing of hurling the highest mountain against a foe; and of men swallowed up
in the depths of the treacherous earth, which
opened to receive them. But from all these
marvellous stories, like the country to which they
belong, there exhales a wild and poetic charm.
Even a stranger feels this influence; and how
much more must a native of this far northern
clime feel penetrated with what the ancients
call so aptly "the genius of the place."

Gradually a certain calm fell on our hero's
troubled soul. As he slowly recovered the
balance of his mind, he no longer thought des-
pairingly of Carine; he could not believe that
she would persist in keeping him at a distance.
He said to himself that she would yet respond
to his love, — that love would create love. He
would make her forget all she had suffered, and
create in her a new soul, a new heart! But he
well knew that with an organization so timid,

delicate, and tender, it would not do to be pre-
cipitate; he must wait until the time came
when she would voluntarily yield. So reasoned
this grand master of female hearts! A ray of
hope, feeble and uncertain, like the first light
of dawn, began to illumine his heart. Courage
returned with hope. He had done almost
nothing since his arrival in Sweden; but now he
returned to his work with new ardor. Labor!
is it not always the great consoler of noble and
valiant natures?

The place where Marius found himself was
in every way propitious to his studies; here he
found all the beauties for which he had come
to study in the North, — the sombre forests,
the severe aspect of the mountains, the grand
vegetation nourished by the snow and the
winter, the rocks with their metallic tints,
and the beautiful cascades leaping from the
mountain's height into the gigantic basins of
granite. He made no more plans; for the
present he drifted. Where could he be better

situated to work and to wait? The " Edda "
passed the Trolhätta every ten days, and
Captain Mandel never went to Gothenburg
without seeing Tegner and his family. Thus
our young friend could often have news of

Carine : was not that what he most desired?
He arranged his time as well as possible, and
began a series of curious studies (which later
on proved very valuable to him). He was not
unhappy, for he was not devoid of hope ; and
even an unrequited love may suffice to fill a

life, — for those who truly love find a charm in mere existence.

The first week proved uneventful, and was passed in the bosom of the most profound solitude that Marius had ever known. He had left the little inn at Trolhätta, for it was too much frequented by English travellers, and their company was distasteful to him. They treated the world like a conquered country, were too arrogant, and were also noisy and blustering, as they often are in strange lands (seeming to look down on all foreigners because, forsooth, they are not English), although they are usually cold and reserved at home. So our hero sought lodgings elsewhere, and established himself at some distance from the village, in the home of a simple peasant, whose good wife thought she was making a golden bargain by renting him half of their cottage at five francs per week. He arranged in an empty granary a studio lighted from the north, with the most admirable and the purest light that the most fastidious artist could desire. When he had worked eight days, and had just finished a beautiful picture of the grand cascade, and was busily criticising it, he looked up and perceived, smiling at the entrance (when he least expected him), his friend Petrus Mandel.

Chapter XVI.

"You are surprised?" said the captain; "and I also. I did not expect to be here so soon; we are twenty-four hours ahead of time, and that for various reasons too long to enumerate."

"And which I am not curious to hear," said Marius, greeting him warmly.

"Very well, then, that suits me. But give me a cigar, and order me a cup of tea; for I

have not taken anything to-day, and we leave
in an hour."

"And Carine?" asked Marius.

"Oh, there *is* some news."

"Wretch! not to have told me!"

"I came as soon as possible."

"You have seen her?"

"No; and I know no one in Gothenburg
at present who sees her."

"I beg you to explain," cried Marius.

"Very well.   Carine has left her uncle's!"

"Gone?"

"You have said it."

"How long since?"

"Four or five days."

"Does any one know where she has gone?"

"Not I, at least."

"Then you have not the details?"

"No; I know only that she is much better."

Marius experienced an indefinable feeling of
well being, — like a drowning man, who has
remained a long time under water, and who

returns to the fresh air and to the sweet light. Now that Mandel had told him all he knew, and he had drawn from him all he could, Marius experienced an imperious desire to be alone. Thus, in spite of his sincere friendship for the young Swede, it was not without a secret pleasure that he saw him draw out his watch, and on perceiving the time take his hat, and, pressing his friend's hand warmly, say, "Adieu, my dear boy. I must go; it will not do to keep my boat waiting." He quickly took his departure.

Marius was now both glad and sorry, — glad to know that Carine was better, and that now he might hope one day to see her in complete health, not only of body but of mind; unhappy, because he knew not where she was, — and for those who love, uncertainty is a bitter torment. Yet he did not wish to return to Gothenburg. He told himself, not without reason, that he had no right to question Tegner, to ask him to unfold family secrets to a stranger, or to try

and force a confidence that had not been given
voluntarily.   If he hoped to learn anything, it
was by the interposition of the captain, who
was a mutual friend, well acquainted with all
the circumstances.

The result of these meditations was that
Marius remained at Trolhätta, and finished
his large picture.   It was a simple study of the
landscape, but was painted in such a free and
powerful style. that on beholding it one in-
stinctively felt the master, for there was genius
in it.   He found, however (was this a lover's
idea, or was it the idea of an artist?), that
without a human figure, animated with life,
Nature was cold and empty.   "A figure would
look so well," thought he, "at the base of this
rock ; there, where the sunlight brightens and
glances over the transparent cascade, there is
the place !"   Our artist was prompt to exe-
cute : with him, to think was to act.   He took
his palette and his brushes, and set to work.

The figure which soon began to appear under

his skilful fingers, — will our readers need to see it, to divine who it was? It was the same which once already, under the light of the family lamp, in face even of the charming model, he had drawn with so much pleasure and interest. The picturesque Dalecarlian costume accorded well with the landscape in the midst of which he painted it; it seemed very natural for him to clothe her in that costume here. The beautiful face which he had drawn more than once before seemed to beam with happiness; for now it was not the careworn, despairing maiden : it was a new Carine, full of youth and life, and bearing on her countenance the brilliant hue of health. It was Carine as she would have been if her cruel destiny — a wicked man — had not destroyed her budding beauty in the morning of her springtime.

Danglade was not a portrait painter, and I dare say a critic might have found some flaw in his picture; but one felt in this work a certain passion and sincerity which art alone cannot give. He had painted the landscape in the open air and from Nature; the portrait in his studio, from memory. Perhaps the result of this was a certain discord in the *ensemble;* some retouches were still necessary to obtain that general harmony without which no picture is perfect. He had a very simple way to arrive at the desired result. It was to take the picture to the same place where he had painted it, and to give to the whole (the sky, the trees, and the rocks) a last touch of the brush, — those supreme retouches which perfect and harmonize a work, even change its quality, and complete the seal of a powerful whole. Marius resolved to complete his work on the spot whence he had taken his *point de vue.*

It was on one of those lovely little islands of Trolhätta, joined to the shore by a picturesque alpine bridge, which shakes and trembles under the passer's feet. Crossing this frail bridge the path leads to the promontory, where our artist had established himself opposite one of the most beautiful of the five cascades. This pathway was surrounded by a dense mass of foliage, which prevented one seeing ten steps ahead, and ended at an immense rock straight as a wall; behind the rock there was a little esplanade, whence the view was beautiful and extensive, taking in the whole majesty of the cataracts. The peasant at whose cottage Marius lodged knew the place well, for there he had often carried his lodger's easel, camp-stool, and canvas, — for the artist called this place his open-air studio. Here he sent his picture, then, for the last time. The honest peasant, not knowing how to set up the canvas, contented himself with placing it at the foot of the easel near the rock; and putting the palette and the box of colors near by he returned to his work, leaving all in God's care, which is sufficient in this neighborhood, where dishonesty is almost unknown, — here especially where men are not numerous.

Marius remained in his room a little later
than usual. At first he had been detained by
Mandel; then he had taken some time to write
letters home to his parents, who had been
sadly neglected since his arrival in Sweden;
lastly, he rested because he had so little to do,
keeping back the moment, like an epicure with
a dainty dish, so as to enjoy it longer, — tasting it in advance. Toward noon he sealed his
letters, locked his trunks, told the peasant to
give him his account and to come after the
picture about four o'clock; then he took the
path to the cascade. He lingered some time
on the border of the torrent, filling his soul
with the grand spectacle offered to his vision,
with concentrated and absorbed attention, —
for he wished to seize all the details, and to
engrave this scene forever on his memory. At
last he crossed the little bridge, and, hastening
his steps, entered the pathway which led to the
esplanade where he had established his observatory. Imagine his astonishment on behold-

ing a woman before his picture! She seemed
to be examining it with profound attention;
that is, he judged so by her attitude, for he
could not see her face. But her bending head,
her arms hanging down full length, — in a
word, her motionless and statue-like form
showed that her whole soul had passed into
her eyes. This woman appeared to be young,
from the *svelte* elegance of her form. She was
very simply clad in a dress of dark stuff. It
was so sombre that it might have passed for a
mourning robe (mourning for her youth and
for her love), and falling by a single plait from
her shoulders to her feet.

Our hero's heart beat violently. What would
he have given to see her eyes, her neck, or
even a floating tress of her hair! But a little
silk fichu which covered her shoulders reached
almost to her ears, and a large straw hat
trimmed with black lace covered her head.
It was impossible to discover who she was at
this distance. At last Marius, whose southern

temperament did not include patience among the number of his virtues, advanced resolutely toward the picture. At the sound of his steps, which he did not try to conceal (for he did not wish to surprise the stranger too suddenly), the unknown turned.

It was Carine !

On seeing the young girl, with a gesture stronger than his will, by an impulse more prompt than his thoughts, Marius held out both arms and bounded toward her. Carine on the contrary, on perceiving him, became deathly pale ; her knees trembled, and she looked around for a support in vain. Danglade approached, took her hand and drew it within his trembling arm.

"Me?" cried Carine in a feeble voice, pointing to the young Dalecarlian seated on a rock in the foreground of the picture. "Me?" repeated she, looking at the artist.

"Yes, you !" replied he, warmly. "Yes, Carine, you ! always you ! Why may I not fill my picture with the image of one who fills my life?"

"Monsieur! Monsieur!" cried the maiden, trying to draw away her hand.

But Marius held it tightly in his, and would not let it go.

Near them was the trunk of a fallen pine-tree, a prostrate giant, the roots of which like long hair floated in the rushing waters. Her lover placed her on this rustic seat and seated himself by her side, still holding tightly her little hand, for he was resolved she should not escape him this time. They were silent a few moments: it was enough for him to look at her for the present. Carine did not speak, and on her beautiful face was an expression of fear, — with which, however, already mingled a little joy.

Marius well understood what tact and delicacy he would need to tame, little by little, this timid gazelle. He began, therefore, by not speaking of themselves; it was without doubt the best way to reassure her. He asked news of Tegner, of her aunt, and of Elfrida. At first greatly troubled, Carine gradually became self-possessed, and soon conversed in a more rational manner than Marius had ever before heard her. When he believed that he had sufficiently put to flight her fears, he gave to their conversation a more intimate tone.

"You were suffering," said he, "when I met you at Gothenburg?"

Perhaps the remembrance of her grief was still too fresh and too bitter, for on hearing these words Carine started from her seat as if stung by a serpent, and essayed to flee; but Marius held her hand tightly, and gently forced her to sit down again and listen to him.

"Why do you wish to fly from me?" said he. "Am I not your friend?"

"My friend!" said Carine, hanging her head with an air of profound melancholy. "You appear to know my history. Well, then, you must know that I have no friends."

"Do not be ungrateful," replied he, still holding her hand. "Yes, I know all," continued he, looking at her fixedly.

"Then you know a sad history," and Carine blushed deeply.

" Yes, sad for him who has made you suffer."

"Oh, do not attack him!" cried she; "that is no consolation to me."

" I know that you have a noble and generous nature; but do you think God wills you to condemn not only yourself but others to perpetual mourning?"

Carine did not reply, but hung her head.

" Because your first experience has been unfortunate," continued he, "is that any reason why you should despair?"

"One loves but once," murmured the maiden.

"And are you sure that you really loved? Is it then really a *serious* love, — this first tender experience of a young heart that hardly knows itself, and, like the wandering shoots of your hop-vines, attaches itself to the first object it meets."

Carine raised her eyes to heaven, — her lovely blue eyes, wet with tears, — as if to call it to witness the injustice of these words, and to prove the ardor and sincerity of the sentiment which had inspired her youth.

"But at present, at least, you do not love him?" asked Marius, anxiously.

"No," replied she, with more firmness than she had yet shown.

"And you cannot live without love?"

Carine blushed and hung her head, and an expression of unspeakable melancholy stole over her face. "The tree struck by a thunderbolt," said she, "bears never again flowers or leaves!"

"Ah, no doubt it is thus when celestial fire has devoured its sap and drained its life; but when it only strikes the branches, then when the springtime comes again it is covered with buds and blossoms, and reclothed with leaves."

The maiden looked at this very persistent youth wonderingly; then blushed, and turned away her head.

"Carine," said Marius, drawing a little nearer, "shall I offend you if I tell you that the first moment I saw you, I was attracted toward you by an ardent sympathy, and that ever since this feeling has increased?"

"Oh, how *can* I believe you? I am so unworthy of such sentiments!"

"That is not the question," said he, smiling; "no one can ever give a *reason* for loving."

Carine became agitated, and her heart beat violently.

"Do you remember," continued he, "the first day I arrived at Gothenburg?"

"Yes; they had spoken of you. I did not come down, for I did not wish to meet a stranger."

"On that day," said Marius, "I heard your name twice. I thought it sweet; it seemed to caress my ear, and stirred some strange feeling in my heart. I had not yet seen you, and yet I was interested in you. Perhaps that was the dawn of my love. The night came. I could not sleep in this strange country where it was always light. Leaning from the balcony, I saw you in the garden ; you seemed to me beautiful as a dream-maiden, — pensive as Melancholy, sad as Niobe. I was young; I had never loved ; and my heart went out into your keeping, — and you have had it ever since."

Carine raised her hand as if to warn him to speak no more.

"The next day," continued the young man, who was not so easily silenced, "the next day I saw you again. From that moment I could not turn away my eyes from your dear face. To me you were the only woman in the world. You were for me a radiant image of beauty. In a word, I loved you. And yet, cruel girl that you were, nothing seemed to touch you ; my attentions seemed to irritate you, and my sympathy for you was only equalled by your antipathy for me."

"Antipathy! Ah, it was necessary to make you think so," cried Carine. "If you had known—"

"Do not fear. I did not know. I was in despair; and as I could not forget you I resolved to fly from you."

"When I knew it," said Carine, with a touching simplicity, "it was too late; you had gone!"

"And you regretted me? Tell me that you missed me!"

"The house seemed very empty," replied the maiden, blushing.

"But I did not lose you entirely," said Marius, "for I carried your image and your name everywhere. The captain of the 'Edda,' Petrus Mandel, is a friend of your family; he knew your history, and I learned it from him."

A vivid blush covered the young girl's face, and she turned away, saying, "He did wrong to tell you."

"Ah, Carine, beloved ! do not blush for thy virtue ; do not blush for the noble and generous devotion of thy soul !" cried her lover, with a fire which he could not master. "Few women have suffered such wrong ; no one has been more basely deceived ; believe me, he was never worthy, — your idol was but clay. I am sure you already perceive that it was a fortunate escape ; you never would have been happy as his wife, for you are his superior in every way. Do not regret these trials out of which you have come purified, and for which God will perhaps permit me to recompense thee with my love."

Carine, a little troubled by the vehemence of the young man, and by his ardent language of passion, such as she had never heard before, — Carine trembled ; but she dared not interrupt him.

"Ah," continued he, "I soon felt that my life was changed ; that I lived for you alone, and that at any cost I must see you once more.

Perhaps you have heard your uncle say that I wished to visit the North, and to penetrate as far as possible those terrible regions where gradually the cold seizes you and slowly freezes your heart. Yes, it was there I wished to go, so as to forget you; but after having heard your history, it was not the north pole that I sought,— it was you ! I begged Mandel to put me on shore, and I took the route to Gothenburg — but slowly. I did not wish to arrive too soon. How did I know, alas! if you desired my return? How could I approach one who appeared resolved to fly from me? How could I speak to one who desired not to listen to me? I disliked speaking to your uncle; there are subjects on which it is better to be silent if one cannot avow them to the person who inspires them. I so much feared a cold reception that though my desire to obtain the end was great, I sought every pretext to loiter on the way. At last, one day's journey from Gothenburg I resolved to make a

14

final halt, and I hoped in some way to receive news of you. To pass the time I painted these trees, these rocks, and these cascades, all which perhaps had seen you pass by in your youthful beauty. Then I invoked my memory. You can see," added he, pointing to the picture, " if my memory was faithful. In my picture you see yourself ! "

" But a hundred times more beautiful ! " cried Carine, secretly flattered by this *chef-d'œuvre* before her eyes. " But," continued she, " to paint thus it is necessary to have great talent."

" No, it suffices to love and — "

" Oh, tell me no more ! "

" Because you know all, — is it not so, dear girl? Because you know very well that I love you? "

A pale rose-flush tinted the maiden's cheeks, like the first rosy light of dawn touching the immaculate whiteness of the snow on the mountain's height.

"Never, never speak of love again!" said she, softly.

"Yes, I will, dear Carine. I will repeat these words, 'I love you, Carine! I love you!' You must accustom yourself to hear them."

"And if I cannot return your love?"

"I ask nothing of you," said he, "only to let me love you, to let me console you. For a long time *you* gave without receiving; for the present, you can receive without giving."

"You believe, then, that I could be so selfish?"

"I forbid you not to be! Believe me always, those who love most have the better part. You need not pity me; I am so happy you ought rather to envy me."

"Dear and generous friend! how can I ever thank you enough?" cried the girl.

"By forgetting the past, by confiding the future to me, dear Carine; by permitting yourself to be happy!"

Marius took both Carine's hands in his, and this time she did not withdraw them. He was very near her, their heads nearly touched; he gently passed his arm around her waist and drew her to him. Carine did not resist, but let her lovely blond head fall on his shoulder. "Dearest," murmured he, caressing her beautiful hair, "will you be my wife, before God and before man, forever?"

"Ah," said she, "that would be too great happiness! I do not deserve it."

"It is not for thee that I pray," said Marius, "it is for myself; for I cannot live without thee, I cannot separate my destiny from thine; and I will make the future so happy that the remembrance of the past will never present itself to thy thoughts."

Carine disengaged one of her hands, and placing it on Marius's forehead murmured, "Oh, it seems that I can feel my heart reborn! Can I ever endure such perfect happiness?"

"Joy never kills," replied her lover. "To-morrow I will go to Lilla-Edet, and I will ask thy father for thee."

"My father is not at Lilla-Edet; we have left that sad place, which recalls so many cruel thoughts. He now lives a mile from here on a little farm which he owns; and he will be so happy to see you; but he will believe, as I do, that it is all a dream."

"A dream which will have no wakening," said Marius, pressing the hand of the beautiful Swede and looking at her tenderly. But he perceived that to this poor soul, so long plunged in the depths of despair, sorrowful thoughts continually returned; and as his desire was at any cost to distract her, he resolved no longer to speak of love, but asked her what she had done after he left her uncle's house.

"I regretted you," replied Carine with an adorable naïveté. Then remembering suddenly where she was she blushed, and said, "'That was not what I meant to say. I was very glad to see you go."

"One is precisely the contrary of the other," said Marius, smiling, "and I am puzzled which to believe."

"Neither one nor the other," said she, shrugging her shoulders. "How stupid men are not to comprehend what we mean, without explanation! Yes, I was at the same time sad and joyous to see you go, — joyous because your presence was a restraint upon me, for I felt that I was learning to love you; and I did not wish —" here she hid her face in her hands. "Sad," continued she, "for it seemed to me that I should never see you again."

Marius's eyes glistened with the sweetest tears that ever moistened a man's eyes. "Now at least tell me all," cried he. "I wish to know all, — before my coming, after my arrival, during my absence, — all, all!"

"*Mon Dieu!* all is almost nothing," replied Carine, alarmed at the profound tenderness he showed. " Know only that you were never indifferent to me. From the first time I saw you I thought you affectionate and good ; my judgment then was disinterested, for I believed myself separated from the world and from life. After a while I could not help seeing that you took an interest in me. My first impulse was to reciprocate ; then fear took possession of me. I feared that a new love would also prove a new misfortune ; and believing that I had yet time, I kept out of your way. A new love, — it horrified me even to think of it ! *I* was then false as *he*, and he had done well to scorn me and to deceive me ; for I was as bad as he if I was capable of so soon forgetting such profound sentiments."

Here the young girl, who had spoken rapidly, paused for breath ; then she continued.

" 'The evening when you drew my picture, — a portrait so admirably done, and which I have looked at many times since, — I felt emotions that I had believed forever dead. But I would not permit myself to think of you; I fled from you; and when by chance I met you, I turned another way. But in spite of all, my friend, when you went away it seemed to me that the world was empty. Dear absent one! I sought you everywhere. I sought your eyes, so many times tenderly fixed on mine, and reproached myself with my coldness to you. I listened for the sound of your steps, and I grieved when I heard them not, for I had learned to distinguish them from all others. I ought to tell you also that in giving a new interest to my life, in creating in me, whether I would or no, a new source of thought, you had done me much good; you taught me that I had more life in me than I supposed. But the remembrance of my first mistake and of my resistance to my parent's will always came between us, and told me that I was not worthy of you, and that I did not deserve the happiness of being a good man's wife. I resolved to fly from the house where you were sure to return. Now,

my friend, you know all; you have judged me,
and I feel that you have pardoned me."

"Ah, what have I to pardon, my beloved?
God himself, who sees the depths of our hearts,
finds thee as pure as the youngest of his angels.
Come, conduct me to your parents. To-day
we will love; we will work to-morrow."

Chapter XVII.

THE end of our story draws near. The father of Carine had already learned about Marius from Tegner, — of the arrival of the young Frenchman at Gothenburg, and of the great interest he had taken in Carine, and of the happy influence he had over her. Therefore our hero was received as a dear friend, and before many days the young couple were betrothed.

In Sweden the ceremony of betrothal, or as we call it in France *fiancailles*, is completely distinct from that of marriage. Between the

first and the second there elapses sometimes
several years. This custom has few inconven-
iences and many advantages; it is like a novi-
tiate of marriage. Gradually the young couple
become accustomed to the grave ideas which
ought to be born of this sacrament; they slowly
awake to life's seriousness, and advance step by
step toward the end which they have so long
contemplated, instead of precipitating themselves headlong toward the irrevocable. They
do not improvise eternal bonds, but tighten the
knot more and more each day, until the hour
when it becomes indissoluble. They replace
the fierceness of love by a peaceful companionship, learning to love each other more by a
mutual understanding. Their manners are purified and refined by this companionship, while
their happiness preserves always the hope of
greater joy. Thus the first years of life are not
deprived of their sweetest charm; the spring-
time of youth is not allowed to remain a
stranger to love, but this preliminary bond,

which nothing can diminish in purity or
strength, preserves the youthful heart from ills
which might otherwise overtake it. Between
the first youth — unreflecting, untrained, and a
little foolish — and life cold, serious, and positive, this custom puts an interval of calm enjoyment, of delightful reflection, and of labor
sweetened by prospective happiness, and these
first years of strength, always restless, pass thus
consoled and serene. When evil hours and
temptations come to a youth, he has at least as
a defence that which is wanting with us, — a
remembrance and a cherished thought; life has
from the first an aim, which becomes its charm;
wisdom is less difficult to follow when one
knows the recompense; and in waiting the time
when he will also be the head of a family, the
young man takes refuge in hope to escape the
solitude of soul, — the worst of all solitudes.
Dreamer by nature, in place of dreaming of an
unknown woman, or doing worse still, he dreams
of the maiden who will one day be his wife.

The *fiancés* have a social position, recognized by law as well as by custom. They cannot break the bond without cause; one cannot dismiss lightly, or repudiate without motive, a faithful *fiancé*. For the rest they enjoy a sufficient liberty; they accept invitations together, and without the family; together they go to the play or to the ball, and they walk together, — *together* and *alone !* — two words which mean much to lovers. No one dares to criticise this, for they know that a woman is never more safe nor more respected than by him who expects one day to be her husband. By giving young girls more liberty an inordinate desire for freedom is prevented, or woman's rights, which compromise in many cases the happiness of homes. In France the women marry more to obtain social position and freedom than for love of their husbands. In Sweden, where they have more to lose than to gain by marriage, they accept the husbands in spite of marriage.

Chapter XVIII.

ONE day Tegner was delighted to welcome
Marius and Carine. But was *this* Carine?
Could one recognize the poor abandoned one
in this brilliant beauty with dazzling smiles,—
beautiful in her happiness? Every one hastened
to congratulate them; and Brask, who was at
the time assisting Elfrida to wind a skein of
silk, was not the last one to wish them joy.

In the mean time Marius had written a long
letter to his father, to explain how he had

fallen in love with a beautiful and amiable girl, and that they were already *fiancés;* that he had not thought to find a wife in Sweden, but that he loved this maiden very much, and knew he would be happy with her. Here followed enthusiastic praises of Carine. He ended by begging his father to permit him to marry her at her uncle's house, before setting out for France.

The father replied : —

"Unfortunate child ! you are the pest of my life. But as you have deserted a noble career of commerce, marry whom you will; any woman is good enough for an artist." [Here allow us to add in parenthesis that the consul had given to Monsieur Danglade the best references in the world of the family of Carine.] "I do not think it was precisely for that I sent you to Sweden, as you say, although I have not the advantage of knowing your future wife; but I had reserved for you here a certain brunette, who is not a beauty, but whose complexion the sun will never harm (unlike your blond), and with whose *dot* you might forever be relieved of the necessity of selling your poor pictures.

"However, bring home your incomparable blonde! I would like to see her. But if she does not prove the marvel you describe, I will send you both to seek your fortunes in Lapland. Tell her I hope she will learn to love her old father-in-law a little, and that I will try to support you both — and even all *three* — next year!"

15

Chapter XIX.

At the end of October, when already the ice descending from the Gulf of Bothnia began to heap up in the entrance of the Belt, "La Walkyrie" made her last trip for the season. At the stern of the vessel a young man and woman enveloped in furs, and like two chilly birds pressed closely against each other, gazed, hand in hand, at the swiftly passing shores of Sweden, — the beautiful fjord where the river Gotha rolls her silver waves, and the noble hills, crowned with oaks and young elms, which rise above the city. The young woman, at the moment when the vessel passed into the open sea, waved a silent adieu to Sweden. She was not sad, — there was on the contrary an expression of happiness in her eyes ; but she was agitated, pensive, and serious, as one always is when for the first time their native land is left behind.

"Dear Carine," said her husband, pressing her close to his heart, "fear nothing. We shall be together, and we will soon return." Then leading her to the other side of the vessel, he pointed southward, saying : "Dearest, there, in that sunny clime, you will find loving hearts to welcome you !"

Carine smiled, and placed her hand in his. Then silently they watched the fast receding shores.